SCANDAL AT THE
SALTY DOG

MURDER STALKS THE COBBLED
STREETS OF PIRATE'S COVE

After elderly recluse Juliet Blackwell suffers
a mysterious fall in her spooky old mansion,
she insists the ghost of long-dead pirate
Rufus Blackwell has come to avenge himself
on the last member of his treacherous clan.

Bookshop owner and occasional amateur sleuth
Ellery Page doesn't believe in ghosts,
but he knows fear when he sees it,
and it's clear to him his eccentric customer
is genuinely terrified.

Who or what is haunting Miss Blackwell,
what, if anything, does it have to do with
mysterious goings-on at the Salty Dog pub—
and why is *any* of it Ellery's problem?

According to Police Chief Jack Carson,
it's *not* Ellery's problem, and just maybe
Ellery should stop asking awkward questions
before it's too late.

SCANDAL AT THE
SALTY DOG

SECRETS & SCRABBLE BOOK FOUR

JOSH LANYON

VELLICHOR BOOKS

An imprint of JustJoshin Publishing, Inc.

SCANDAL AT THE SALTY DOG: AN M/M COZY Mystery
(Secrets and Scrabble Book 4)
June 2021
Copyright (c) 2021 by Josh Lanyon
Edited by Keren Reed
Cover and book design by Kevin Burton Smith
All rights reserved.

ISBN: 978-1-945802-66-9
Published in the United States of America

JustJoshin Publishing, Inc.
3053 Rancho Vista Blvd.
Suite 116
Palmdale, CA 93551
www.joshlanyon.com

*This is a work of fiction. Any resemblance to persons living or
dead is entirely coincidental.*

To Jordan Lombard. Thank you for your energy, your enthusiasm, your engagement, and everything else..

Sailor, waken, death is near,
Waken from deceitful sleep;
Sailor, ere the dawn appear,
Thou shalt slumber in the deep.

"The Pirate-Ship," William Bingham Tappan

CHAPTER ONE

Ellery Page was dreaming of New York.

He was standing in line, though whether for theater tickets or Absolute Bagels was unclear, when the person behind him leaned in and kissed the back of his neck.

Ellery's eyes popped open. He was not in line. He was not in New York. He was in bed at Captain's Seat, the decrepit mansion he'd inherited from his Great-great-great-aunt Eudora a few months earlier. The eighteenth century portrait of a life-sized Captain Horatio Page gazed down at him with a dubious expression.

"Better get a move on. You're going to be late."

That opinion was not offered by Captain Horatio Page. That was Pirate Cove's police chief and Ellery's, well, boyfriend, Jack Carson.

Ellery turned his head to answer, and his face was immediately covered in wet, passionate kisses. That was also not Captain Horatio Page. Nor, sadly, Jack. That was Watson, Ellery's sixish-month-old black spaniel mix puppy and occasional (according to Jack) partner in crime.

Ellery started to laugh, kissed Watson back—though less passionately. "Good morning to you too."

Jack bent to scoop up Watson at the same moment Ellery sat up, and their near collision resulted in a kiss that went on a little longer than either anticipated, ending in smiles and reluctant parting of lips.

As Jack drew back, Ellery realized he was already dressed, right down to his police boots. That navy-blue uniform really suited Jack's athletic six feet, one hundred and ninety-plus pounds and rugged good looks.

"Yikes. I really *am* late." Ellery threw back the sheet and summer blanket.

"No. I'm early. I've got breakfast with the State Police Superintendent."

Ellery's smile was wry. "That's right. And dinner with the town council." He was learning fast that Always in Demand was part of Jack's job description.

"I could meet you for dessert?"

"Silver Sleuths. I promised Nora I'd look in." This was Ellery's first day, his first official day, back at work after suffering what Jack referred to as an *extracurricular* concussion. Amateur sleuthing turned out to be a hazardous hobby. Not that Ellery viewed his sleuthing as a hobby. Or even something he planned on doing again.

Jack considered. "What are you doing tomorrow night?"

"You tell me."

Jack grinned, leaned in to kiss him one final time, and murmured, "I will. In detail."

Definitely a great way to start what promised to be a very busy morning.

Less great, although he was eagerly looking forward to being cleared for action, was having to stop by Buck Island Med Center on the way into work.

BIMC was located in a mid-century former mansion, so from the outside, the building had a cozy look to it. Inside, it was like any other vacation spot emergency facility.

Even at that time of the morning, the medical center was packed with visitors suffering (loudly) from sunburns, sprains, and stings. Buck Island in summer was a different world from Buck Island the rest of the year. Business was about a thousand percent better—for everyone—but Ellery couldn't help missing the peace and quiet of the island he now thought of as home, dreams of New York notwithstanding.

He checked in at the front desk and spent a few minutes sitting in the waiting room with unfamiliar people complaining about hangovers, food poisoning (likely more hangovers), how no one on the island could drive, the island's fascist police force, and then finally, mercifully, he was buzzed through to the examination room.

He was a little disappointed when Ione Jay, the center's senior nurse practitioner, greeted him. Not that he didn't like Ione, but he'd sort of been hoping to see Dr. Mane again. Largely because he'd been wondering if the doctor was quite the character he'd seemed when Ellery had been suffering from concussion.

Ione was a stocky, sensible-looking woman, whom Ellery mostly knew from open mic at the Salty Dog pub. Ione belted out soul songs from the sixties with an easy and enviable aplomb.

Ellery was able to assure Ione he was no longer suffering from dizziness, fatigue, headaches, or ringing in his ears. She examined what was left of his dissolvable stitches, complimented him on the beauty of the wound healing on the back of his skull, and pronounced him fit to return to work.

"We're back in business, buddy," Ellery informed Watson when he climbed back into the VW parked in a shady corner of the crowded parking lot.

Watson grinned and wagged his tail in approval.

A short time (and several close calls with speeding golf carts later) Ellery arrived at the Crow's Nest and parked in the tiny lot behind the bookshop.

He had stopped to pick up pastries from Long Johns and Jelly Rolls, and he had to balance the box and hang onto Watson's leash—Watson having decided he simply *had* to meet the Chihuahua hurling abuse from across the street—as he unlocked the front door.

He managed to get the door open without dropping a single pastry, and stepped inside the bookshop.

As always, his heart lightened at the sight of green-gold light from the sunlit harbor flooding through the bay corner windows, gilding the book bindings and old picture frames. The polished wooden floors glowed. Vintage ships' lanterns, lining the back wall, blinked and winked in cheerful *welcome back*!

He nodded good morning to Rupert, the resin skeleton in pirate costume, who resided in the glass case at the end of a row of bookshelves. Rupert laughed silently back, perhaps amused at the idea of working in a bookshop when one could be marauding on the open seas. Not that there was much of a living to be made marauding these days or at least in these seas.

It was funny to think that at this time last year, he (that would be Ellery, not Rupert) hadn't even known this place existed. Had no idea there was such a place as Buck Island or Pirate's Cove. Hadn't even known he had a great-great-great-aunt Eudora, let alone that he was in line to inherit a failing bookstore and the falling down family mansion.

And now?

Now the bookstore was, well, maybe not a *roaring* success, but it was still afloat. With Jack's help, Captain's Seat was slowly, very slowly, being restored to, maybe not its former glory, but certainly something more than habitable. And then there was Jack himself.

The thought of Jack made Ellery smile, but the thing between them still felt so new, so fragile, he didn't want to...handle it too much. Didn't want to overthink it. But so far so good. In fact, so much better than he had even hoped.

"Good morning!"

Ellery had smelled coffee brewing when he opened the door, so he was not startled when Nora popped out of an aisle of bookshelves.

"Morning!"

On paper, Nora Sweeny was his assistant, but really, she was so much more. Not only was Nora more knowledgeable about mysteries and bookselling than Ellery, she had grown up on the island and seemed familiar with everyone—and everyone's most dearly held secrets. She was a slight but sturdy seventy-something New Englander, and though barely five feet tall, impossible to overlook. Her eyes were gray and piercing. Nora saw all and had an opinion on everything.

"You look very pleased with the world this morning," she observed.

"I am," Ellery said. "I was going stir-crazy at home."

Nora, unsnapping Watson's leash from his collar, diplomatically didn't point out that Ellery had been on the phone and the computer for the past three days, trying to manage the bookshop remotely.

"Well, it's wonderful to have you back."

"Thanks. It's wonderful to be back." He held up the flat box. "I brought pastries to celebrate."

Nora looked disconcerted. "*Oh.* That was thoughtful. So did I!"

"Oops. Oi, Innkeep! Carbs for all!"

They grinned at each other.

Ellery set his box beside Nora's pink one on the wooden counter. "No worries. Felix will eat them."

Felix Jones, son of Pirate Cove's former mayor, was temporarily helping out in the bookshop while Ellery recuperated. His former girlfriend, Libby Tulley, had also been helping out, but a week earlier Libby's dad, Tom, owner of the Salty Dog pub, had been stricken with a burst appendix.

Fortunately, Tom was now on the mend, recovering at home, but that left Libby to try and manage the pub during their busiest and rowdiest season.

"Nonsense," Nora said. "We'll dole them out to our first customers. Buy two books and get a free doughnut."

Ellery said admiringly, "You really *are* descended from pirates!"

Nora's sniff was close to a snort. She changed the subject. "We've received some replies to your online job posting."

"Already? That's great."

Nora's murmur was noncommittal.

"*Isn't* it great?"

Initially Ellery had resisted the idea of hiring more help for the bookshop, but sales had risen during the two weeks he'd been dry-docking. Partly that was because July was the height of Pirate Cove's business season, but partly, having enough staff did make a big difference to the efficient running of the Crow's Nest. So, while it was kind of a relief that his temporary help were no longer circling each other like two cats trapped in a box, and despite Nora's assurances that they could manage without Libby, Ellery knew they did need more help at the bookshop. At least during the summer season.

Nora definitely had a funny expression. Ellery asked cautiously, "How many replies?"

"Oh. Well…about a hundred."

Ellery's jaw dropped. He repeated, "A hundred?"

"Give or take."

"We have one hundred applicants to sort through?"

Nora said reassuringly, "I don't suppose it will take that long to whittle them down."

"You *don't*?"

"No, dearie. I suspect some of these people don't realize the job is on Buck Island."

That was a good thought. Ellery relaxed. "That's probably true."

"I have no doubt it's true. It's worrying how few people take the time to read the fine print. Or even the large print."

Ellery, occasionally guilty of that himself, made no comment.

"I'll show you mine if you show me yours." He flipped open the white pastry box from Long Johns and Jelly Rolls.

Nora opened the lid of her rectangular box, offering a glimpse of colorful doughnuts in mouthwatering rows. "I'll get the coffee."

"Great. And then you can catch me up on everything."

"There's not so much as you might think. Things have been surprisingly quiet with you out of action."

While Nora got their coffee, Ellery watched Watson busily sniffing every corner of the shop, checking for lurking cats or, worse, mouthy Chihuahuas.

"How's Felix doing?"

Nora, busy at the vintage tea cart they now used as a coffee station for customers, replied, "It's difficult for him, naturally. Once he's away at college, he'll be much happier."

Ellery hoped so. He couldn't help feeling somewhat to blame for Felix's unhappiness. Inevitably, there was always going to be more than one victim in a murder investigation.

Nora returned with two steaming mugs of coffee and handed one to Ellery. "Cheers." She clinked her mug against his. "Welcome back. No more getting conked on the head."

"Thanks. I'll do my best." He sipped his coffee and added, "I blame you."

"*Me?*"

"If you hadn't encouraged my poking into other people's business—"

"Amateur sleuthing."

"Interfering in police business, per Jack."

Nora sniffed disdainfully.

"I would never have wound up concussed in a crypt."

"Mausoleum, dearie. And you didn't *wind up* there, fortunately. Because here you are, safe and sound."

"Which is how I'd like to keep it."

"It's a lesson to us all," Nora said piously, and gave him a brisk pat on the back.

Two cups of coffee, one doughnut, and one jelly roll later, Ellery was at his desk, sorting through the alarming queue of job applicants filling his inbox.

He was pretty sure Nora was right about most of these people not realizing where the job was located. He was also pretty sure she was right about people not bothering to read, well, anything. Starting with the application instructions.

At least this one has *a photo*, he thought, studying the grainy pic of a studious-looking young woman. It was amazing how many applicants left the default gray-and-white silhouette in place. *Does not follow directions* was kind of an immediate disqualifier for most employers. He skimmed the Introduction section and the words *married to books* stood out. Points for enthusiasm. If true, working at the Crow's Nest could be a match made in heaven for... He glanced at the name on the file (they were all starting to run together): Shirley Schreiber.

Unfortunately—or perhaps, fortunately, Ellery hadn't decided yet—what followed was barely enough background information to fill even a third of the single-page file. Judging from the enlarged photo in the top left corner, a quick resize would reduce the text portion to less than half a page. He deduced Shirley was still of the fudging-college-essays age.

Or, given the graininess of that photo, maybe the fudging-high-school-essays age.

He sympathized. There weren't a ton of summer jobs on the island that didn't involve scooping ice cream or flipping burgers. In fact, there weren't a lot of jobs on the island for young adults, period. Many of the businesses were family owned and operated by generations of kith and kin.

He sighed, closed the browser tab, and moved on to the next application.

"I'm kind of unnerved we received nearly a hundred applications just in the first two days."

Nora, who had ears like a bat, confirmed his thoughts from the sales desk.

"Working here would be a dream job for a lot of people."

"Barring the occasional murder."

"Pshaw. We haven't had a murder *here* in months."

"Not in the shop, no. Thankfully."

She appeared in the doorway of his office, holding what looked like a black and gold deck of cards.

"Playing solitaire?" Ellery asked.

Nora beamed and held up the object. "Not at all! This is a vintage Miniature Sherlock Holmes, 1983, Mosaic Press. It's in lovely condition. We can probably get anywhere from one twenty-five to two hundred for it."

"*Nice.* Where did it come from?"

"Imelda Appleby dropped it off with a box of books she put together when she was clearing out her auntie's cottage."

"Ah." Probably twenty percent of their stock was "gifted" one way or the other by members of the community. Ellery went back to skimming names. "Hey, it looks like Jane Smith applied."

Jane was a regular customer and a sporadic member of the Silver Sleuths book club. In Ellery's opinion, that was two points in her favor. He was surprised when Nora pursed her lips, considered, and then shook her head.

"I don't think she would really suit us, dearie."

"You don't?"

"No."

"I didn't realize you didn't like Jane."

"Oh, I like Jane." Nora seemed sincere about that. "But she has a habit of wandering out of the shop without paying. I think that reluctance to part with cash would be an unfortunate tendency in a business where small sums of money change hands regularly."

"When you put it like that..."

"It's nothing against Jane."

Ellery's brows rose.

But Nora insisted, "We all have our weaknesses. My philosophy is, it's better to help people avoid temptation."

"Okay. I'm convinced."

He was. He trusted Nora's opinion; and he too had noticed Jane Smith's almost physical reluctance to let go her cash. Even when it was no longer her cash.

In any case, the cheery tinkle of the bell on the front door signaled the first prospective customer of the day, and Nora departed.

Or maybe not. A second later Nora was back—and Libby was right behind her.

Libby was a cute and personable redhead, but the last couple of months had been rough on her, and her usual bright smile had been largely MIA the last month or so. It was definitely nowhere to be seen that morning.

Nora's expression was worth a thousand words, all of them unnecessary, as it turned out, because Ellery got the message the minute Libby opened her mouth and said in an dangerously high and wobbly voice, "Can I talk to you?"

Uh-oh.

"Of course." Ellery jumped up, came around the desk, and lifted a stack of very dusty 1940s *Ellery Queen's Mystery Magazines* off the wooden chair.

Nora gave him a commiserating look and withdrew, like a silver wraith, from his office. Libby unfairly blamed Nora for a good portion of her romantic woes, which Nora bore stoically.

Libby dropped into the wooden chair, whispered, "Felix isn't here, is he?"

"No. He doesn't come in until eleven."

She already knew that, of course, so she had to be stalling. He waited uneasily.

Libby chewed her lip, said, "Promise you won't laugh at me."

This was getting weirder and weirder. Ellery assumed whatever it was, it had to do with Libby's complicated love life, which he truly did not want to be involved in, but he said solemnly, "I won't laugh."

She let out a long breath. "Ellery, I want to hire you as a…a detective."

CHAPTER TWO

Ellery laughed.

"*Ellery!*"

He put his hands up in apology. "Sorry. Sorry, I just… I'm not a detective, Libby. You know that."

"Yes, you are. You're just not a professional. You're not the police. Which is good. Because I *hate* the police." Her eyes filled with tears, and her cheeks grew very pink.

Ellery sighed. He knew perfectly well what *that* was about. "Come on. It's not fair to be mad at Jack. Jack's only doing his job. If you want to be mad at someone, be mad at your—"

He stopped as the first tears trickled down her cheeks.

"This isn't about—" Libby broke off, struggled, and said more calmly, "This isn't anything to do with *that*. This is about the Salty Dog."

He heard this news with relief. For one alarming moment he had feared she was going to ask him to try and clear the very guy who had knocked him over the head two weeks earlier. "Okay. What about the Salty Dog?"

"There's something going on. Something wrong, I mean."

"Like what?"

"I don't know."

Interesting but not helpful.

He opened his mouth, but she said quickly, "That is, I don't know what it *means*. But someone's getting in at night. After hours. After we're closed and everything is locked up. Someone is sneaking inside."

"Sneaking inside and...what?"

"Stealing food out of the fridge. Taking money. Moving things around."

Ellery frowned. "It has to be one of the guests. The upstairs rooms are all rented out during the summer. It has to be a guest."

"It's not a guest."

"But—"

"It's not a guest," she insisted. "There's only one stairway, and a security camera is aimed straight at it. There's no elevator. There are no back stairs."

A fire marshal's nightmare. Like most of the old buildings on the island.

"Okay, but—"

"There's no possible way anyone could get downstairs without showing up on the security camera."

"How do you think they're getting in, then?"

She shook her head, but she'd obviously been thinking about it a lot, because she began to tick the possibilities off her fingers. "There are three security cameras. One is trained on the front entrance, one is trained on the back entrance, and the third one faces the stairs. No one can come downstairs without showing up on that camera, and there's no one on the security footage. I've looked and looked. There's no one there."

"Okay. What about the tunnels?"

"What tunnels?"

"The old system of tunnels beneath the village. Maybe one of the tunnels leads to the Salty Dog?" The pub was certainly old enough to be part of the original network. The tunnels had been built in the late 1600s for purposes of defense—during World War II they had been fitted for use as bomb shelters—but had mostly been used for smuggling and other nefarious occupations.

"Oh. No. There was an entrance to one of the tunnels, but my dad sealed it off when I was little. He was afraid I might wander in and get lost."

"Are you sure about that?"

"Yes. I can show you the bricked-up section in the kitchen. It's been sealed off for years."

That was disappointing.

"If that's true, then by process of elimination, your intruder has to be coming in through one of the other entrances."

"Maybe."

Ellery frowned. "*Maybe?* Do you have another theory?"

She seemed to avoid his gaze. "You know the pub is supposed to be haunted, right?"

This time he remembered he'd promised not to laugh. "Yeah, but that's true of practically every building in the village."

Slight exaggeration. But only slight. Pirate legends and ghost stories were among the island's natural resources.

Libby said nothing.

Ellery tilted his head, studying her. "You're not really suggesting a ghost is getting in and stealing food from the fridge?"

She admitted grudgingly, "No."

"Because as far as I know, ghosts don't need food. Or money."

"That's why it doesn't make sense."

That's why it didn't make sense? Because otherwise it *did* make sense to her?

Ellery said slowly, "So what you're saying is, no one is showing up on *any* of the security cameras?"

"*Yes.*" She looked relieved that he was *finally* getting the message.

"How would that be possible?"

"Well, if they crawled."

"If they..."

She said eagerly, "Crawled. Right. Pop insisted on installing the security system himself, and the way he positioned the cameras, if someone came in through the front and ducked down and crawled across the floor, they wouldn't be seen on camera."

A whole new meaning to the term *pub crawl*. But wouldn't that be a lot of trouble and a lot of risk to steal some leftovers? The food at the Salty Dog was good, but it wasn't so good anyone would risk jail time to learn the secret to Tom's baked mac-and-cheese casserole. Salt. Salt was the secret ingredient, and you didn't need to see the recipe to know it. Also, if Tom kept more than fifty bucks in petty cash on hand, Ellery would be astonished.

He kept those thoughts to himself, saying only, "But the camera would pick up the door opening. And the security alarm would go off."

"The alarm would go off," Libby agreed. "But if someone knew the code…"

"But again, the camera would pick up the door opening."

Libby hesitated, admitted, "It depends on the shadows in the room."

"You're kidding me."

She moved her head in negation. "At this time of year, between three and five a.m., the front door is too deep in shadow to see if it opens or not."

"But the motion detector—"

"There is no motion detector."

"How can that be?"

Her expression grew a little defensive. "Pop got a great deal on the system because it was being phased out. It was only later on we realized why it was being phased out."

It took Ellery a few seconds to think of a suitable response. "Okay. That's…pretty concerning. But someone would have to know all this. Correct? Because most people would assume you've got a functioning security system."

"Yes. I guess."

"And what about the back entrance?"

"You can't see the door open because it's down that little hallway. But the only way out of the hallway would be on camera. So you would see them even if they were crawling."

Ellery closed his mind to the idea of a gang of crawling burglars. "Right. Therefore, your intruder has to be coming in through the front. And this intruder has to be someone who knows the security code and knows that at certain times of night, the camera won't pick up the motion of the door opening."

"Yeees," she said doubtfully.

He didn't blame her for being doubtful. He was doubtful too. He also couldn't help wondering if there was a chance Libby was making all this up.

With Tom stuck at home, could anyone confirm that there was money and food missing?

Or, if money was missing, maybe Libby had taken it herself?

Damn. Ellery didn't want to think that way, but Libby had been under a huge amount of stress lately. And as hard as it was to believe that she would make up such a preposterous story—let alone steal from her father—was it harder to believe than the notion of mysterious crawling nocturnal intruders?

He kept his tone neutral. "Have you told your dad about any of this?"

"No," Libby said quickly. "No way. If I tell Pop, he's going to insist on coming back to work. He's going to insist he can take care of this himself. And he *can't*." Her eyes welled again. "He has to take it easy until he's recovered." She swallowed. "He almost *died*."

Ellery sympathized. At her age it was natural to believe your parents were immortal, so finding out they were just as vulnerable as everyone else was bound to be a shock. And maybe that shock was driving her to...make up stories for attention?

Was this some kind of kooky cry for help?

"Listen, Libby, are you one hundred percent sure this isn't—that maybe you forgot how much money was in the till?"

"No! I didn't forget! Money is missing. An unopened bottle of Woodford Reserve Double Oaked Bourbon is *gone*."

She was adamant, so he backed off, although he still had his doubts. How could he not?

"Can you think of anyone who would want to frighten or harass you this way?"

"Why would they?"

Not exactly reassuring. "You don't sound sure about that."

"Well"—her voice wavered on the word—"if someone *did* want revenge, I guess this would be one way to get it."

"Who the heck do you think might want revenge on you?"

"No one," she said quickly, unconvincingly.

"Felix?"

"No!"

"Ned?"

She hesitated. "He's in jail. How could he be involved?"

Good question. So why the hesitation?

"Person or persons unknown?"

"This isn't funny, Ellery."

"No, of course not. I'm not really joking. *Do* you really think some unknown person is trying to scare you?"

"I don't know. But I *am* scared. It just seems so...random."

Random was exactly right. The randomness was part of what made it so baffling.

"Has the intruder left you any messages? Notes or phone calls or soap on mirrors?"

She shuddered. "No."

Ellery was silent, considering everything Libby had said—and everything she had not said. He couldn't help thinking there had to be a simple explanation.

SCANDAL AT THE SALTY DOG   31

"Are you sure there's no other way for the B&B guests to get downstairs? Because that explanation still makes the most sense."

"No. The stairs are the only way up or down. We're non ADA because of the age and architecture of the building."

"Right. But what about a service elevator? What about a dumbwaiter?"

"No. I *told* you. There's only way up or down, and the camera facing the staircase is exactly angled to catch anyone trying to sneak downstairs."

"Okay, but that's a lot of footage to—"

She didn't let him finish. "I know it is! I've watched hours and hours and *hours* of recording. I haven't slept for two nights because I keep watching the at-home monitor to see if I could spot anything."

If true, that explained a lot. There was nothing like lack of sleep to drive you bonkers. If she had convinced herself something spooky was happening at the pub, then maybe Libby was simply a victim of her own active imagination. He definitely preferred that scenario to the Pathological Liar Libby scenario, the Libby in Jep scenario, and, particularly, the Weirdo Pub Crawlers scenario.

"Okay. I believe you. And I want to help. But I'm not exactly sure how I'd do that."

She gave him a blinding smile. "I'm not worried about that!"

He smiled too, though it was forced. "Well, I appreciate the confidence, but *I* am."

He was trying his best to tell her no, but some-how, she was translating his hemming and hawing into yes. In fact, she even laughed. "Oh, Ellery. I know you'll figure it out. This is *nothing* compared to your other cases."

"Yeah, but see, that's my point. I don't actually have cases because I'm not actually—"

He did try.

He was still trying as she hugged him, thanked him, and hurried out of his office.

"**O**h dear," Nora murmured after the shop door slammed shut behind Libby with a discordant bell jangle.

"To put it mildly." Ellery joined her at the front desk.

"The child does need help."

"Well, yes. I get that. And at the risk of sounding like a broken record, I do want to help, but—"

BUT was the subject, the verb, and the object of that unfinished sentence.

Why did no one hear the BUT? Why was no one listening to him?

Nora cut in, "And she's quite right, of course. About Tom coming straight back to work if he catches wind of this."

"I appreciate that. And, like I said, I want to help. *But* I'm not at all sure that humoring her is the best way to do that."

"Humoring her?" Nora looked surprised. "Then you don't believe her story?"

Ellery did a double take. "Do you?"

"It's a very odd thing to make up."

"It's a very odd thing to be true."

"Well...agreed."

Ellery said, "If she's not making it up, then I really have no clue how to help her. I'm *not* a detective."

Nora seemed to be nodding her agreement, but what she said was, "Maybe not officially."

Ellery blinked. "*Maybe* not officially?"

"And you're certainly not a night watchman." Nora added comfortingly, "But there's probably a very simple explanation here."

"Yes. It's the Case of the Midnight Munchies. One of the guests is climbing out their bedroom window, sneaking into the kitchen for a midnight snack, and climbing back in their bedroom window."

"Maybe not that simple."

Ellery grimaced. "Probably not." Another unpleasant thought occurred. He said gloomily, "Also, Jack is not going to like this."

"Very likely not." Nora considered and discarded a couple of answers before beginning delicately, "Of course, Libby did ask you to keep this confi—"

"No way. I am *not* lying to Jack. Not even by omission."

"No, no. Of course not." Nora's expression was regretful.

Neither of them spoke as they watched Watson chasing his tail. When the puppy finally fell over, Ellery said, "He's going to miss playing on the beach all day."

"Along with someone else?" Nora teased.

Ellery shook his head. "No. I like working. I missed being at the Crow's Nest."

Nora considered Watson, who was eyeing his tail with deep suspicion.

"Why don't you take him for a little walk? Juliet Blackwell's books came in yesterday. She was hinting on the phone she hoped you'd deliver them."

"You're smirking," Ellery said.

"No, no. Not at all," Nora assured him.

Juliet Blackwell had recently become one of their very best customers. The elderly woman lived in one of the old mansions on the bluffs overlooking Pirate's Cove.

She was—meaning, according to Nora—moody, reclusive, and eccentric. Given that eccentric was kind of a full-time occupation in Pirate's Cove, Ellery thought there had to be more to Miss Blackwell's backstory than he'd heard so far. She did seem pretty much a recluse, though. He'd never seen her outside the Black House. Everything from groceries to books was delivered right to her doorstep.

To her doorstep and no farther.

Maria McGillicuddy "charred" for Miss Blackwell a couple of times a month, Patty Bourbon of Bourbon Street Salon visited weekly for shampoos and manicures, but no one else was ever admitted inside the Black House until two months ago when Ellery had unexpectedly been invited to cross the threshold for *coffee and conversation.*

Actually, it had been for something called "pirate's coffee," which included healthy measures of spiced rum and (Ellery knew his cocktail ingredients) Kahlúa Especial.

That was the reason behind Nora's smirk. Miss Blackwell had, in Nora's opinion, *taken a shine* to Ellery.

"Come on, spit it out," Ellery said.

"She's smitten," Nora informed him, to which Ellery rolled his eyes.

"She's lonely for sure."

"That's her own choice." That seemed rather hard-hearted for Nora, which further spiked Ellery's curiosity.

In all honesty, he'd have preferred simply dropping Miss Blackwell's monthly order of books on her doorstep and departing. A little bit of Miss Blackwell went a long way. Not only did she make him uncomfortable, although he wasn't exactly sure why, she kept trying to ply Watson with rum, no matter how many times Ellery asked her not to.

"She's a good customer, and I don't mind dropping the books off," he said. "Watson, want to go for a walk?"

Watson thought that was a fantastic idea, and in short order, Ellery had Watson back in his little red harness, and was strolling down the seafront walk. During the summer, the visitors outnumbered Pirate Cove's residents about three to one. It seemed as though everyone they passed was lugging a surfboard, carrying a shopping bag, or sipping overpriced coffee.

Ellery glanced inside the brown paper shopping bag stamped with their brand-new Crow's Nest logo. He was very proud of those recyclable shopping bags. They looked so...professional. He studied the books.

Miss Blackwell's taste ran to classic Golden Age puzzlers. Having exhausted Agatha Christie's backlist, she was making inroads on Mary Roberts Rinehart. This month's order included *The After House*, *The Album*, *The Wall*, and *The Great Mistake*.

Poison for profit was Nora's summation. Ellery had not read these books—and had no plans to read them. He much preferred contemporary fiction.

Anyway, it was a gorgeous day for a walk, and he was feeling content.

Occasionally, a golf cart came whizzing around a corner, and Ellery and Watson had to leap out of the way. The third time this happened, Watson scared the lights out of Ellery by lunging for the golf cart. Ellery yanked him back in time and gave him a very stern talking to. Watson listened, solemnly watching Ellery with his big brown eyes—and then licked Ellery's nose.

"Yeah, but I mean it," Ellery said, mopping his nose on his shoulder.

Watson was already off again, tugging determinedly at this leash as though descended from a long line of sled dogs.

Beacon Tower Road led off to the west. Ellery and Watson followed the winding dirt lane past a tall stone tower built in 1924 as a memorial to the island and its seamen. This was the highest point on the island. The local Manissean tribe held council on the bluff, and from Colonial days through the Revolution and the War of 1812, islanders kept oil-soaked logs there to light up as a warning to their neighbors that enemy ships were approaching.

Bees hummed, and the earth was warm and fragrant with the smell of dust and Queen Anne's lace.

From this vantage point, Ellery could gaze down at the chimneys and rooftop of Bloodworth Manor House against the blue backdrop of Old Harbor. This time of year, the harbor was filled with sailboats and cabin cruisers, like giant seagulls bobbing on the waves.

He spared a thought for Julian and Marguerite Bloodworth. Last he'd heard, mother and son were in New York, with no plans to return to Buck Island in the near future. Which, frankly, was a relief.

At last Ellery and Watson reached the massive iron gates that separated the Blackwell property from the rest of the world.

Like most of the island's grand old houses, the Black House was nearly invisible behind a carefully cultivated bower of trees, but Ellery could see the glint of windows in the cupola. Much of the original structure had burned in 1880 and been replaced by a classic Queen Anne with salty shingles, rising gables, and wraparound porch.

There was argument within the historical society as to whether "the Black House" qualified as one of the original Pirate's Eight. Most of the island's stately manors, i.e., former pirate fortresses, had been built in the 1600s. Rufus Blackwell had been the last of the island's "great" pirates, and construction on the Black House had only been completed in 1720. Three years before Rufus had been hung in Newport along with twenty-five other, er, colleagues.

Miss Blackwell was the last of Rufus's descendants.

Ellery pushed on the gates and realized they were locked.

That was a first.

He considered this unexpected barrier for a perplexed moment or two. Despite the forbidding height and narrow bars, the gates weren't really much of an impediment. The stone wall surrounding the property was only about chest high. Ellery left the gates and walked along until he found a likely spot. He set the bag of books atop the wall, picked up Watson, set him on the wall too, then hauled himself up. He balanced briefly on the narrow ledge and jumped down into the soft grass. Watson, showing uncharacteristic caution, waited to be lifted down.

Ellery retrieved the bag of books and walked on, until he came to the patterned brick walk.

He reached the porch, and made his way through weathered furniture covered in sun-faded canvas.

From inside the house, he could hear Miss Blackwell screaming.

CHAPTER THREE

For a couple of vital seconds Ellery stood paralyzed.

Which was a normal reaction, really, given that he was not action-hero material, even if he had played one—sort of—on the big screen.

Miss Blackwell stopped screaming. The silence that followed was even more terrifying.

Ellery tried the door handle. It was locked. He pounded on the wooden surface, shouting, "Miss Blackwell? Miss Blackwell, are you in there?"

Which was a pretty silly question. He amended that to, "Miss Blackwell? Are you okay?"

Which again, was probably rhetorical.

The sinister hush persisted. He could hear insects buzzing in the warm summer air, hear Watson panting after the long, hot walk, hear the anxious thump of his own heart.

Ellery dropped the book bag, double looped Watson's leash around the curlicue of a cast iron patio chair, and sprinted down the length of the porch, stopping to knock on windows and peer through the grimy glass at the gloomy interior. No one responded to his rapping, and he did not see anything amiss. Granted, he did not see much of *anything*. It seemed Maria McGillicuddy did not do windows.

When he got to the back of the house, he found a half-open window. Lace curtains fluttered languidly in the breeze.

He pushed the window sash all the way up and looked inside.

A multitude of white cabinetry trimmed in black, ceiling-high built-in shelves crowded with canned goods and jars, and miscellany...old-fashioned appliances. He deduced the window was over a sink, and hoisted himself up for a better look.

Yes. The window was over a large farm sink in the kitchen. He could see an enormous range cooker, open dressers, and a long farm table that could have doubled for a runway.

No sign of anything amiss.

"Hello? Miss Blackwell?" Ellery called. "It's me. Ellery Page."

Not so much as the squeak of a floorboard in reply.

"Hello? Miss Blackwell? Don't be afraid. I brought your books."

Now there spoke a bookseller. *Have no fear, your books are here!*

He didn't believe there was any response, although it was hard to know for certain, given the ruckus Watson was making at the front of the house. Hysterical barking was accompanied by the alarming scrape of iron on wood as the pup tried to follow him through the maze of old furniture.

Arf. Arf. Arf.

It was a tight fit, but Ellery was able to climb awkwardly through the window, his tennis-shoe shod foot knocking several tiny china figurines off the sill. His knee took out a crystal wineglass and a small terracotta pot with a long-dead plant. They smashed to bits on the floor, and Ellery swore quietly.

If Miss Blackwell was not in dire straits, she was going to be very unhappy with him.

On the whole, he preferred her irate to in dire straits.

He crammed himself the rest of the way through the window, sending more dishes and wineglasses to their doom, jumped off the counter, and crossed the floor to the hallway.

When he reached the doorway, he hesitated.

"Hello? Miss Blackwell? Can you hear me?"

Since getting knocked over the head, he had developed a greater reluctance for charging into unknown places and situations.

Something was definitely off. The house had a weird listening feel to it.

Arf. Arf. Arf.

Stepping into the grand foyer, Ellery spared a quick, uneasy look for the long, shadowy room. He was relieved to see Miss Blackwell was not lying at the foot of the wide staircase. Frankly, that had been his first guess.

He turned his attention to the staircase itself. With its intricate woodwork and giant Tiffany-inspired stained-glass window, the structure was a work of art. But one slip of the foot and it would be like falling down a small cliff.

A door slammed, and he jumped as though it had been a gunshot.

Arf. Arf. Arf. Arf. Arf. Arf.

Where had that sound come from? Between Watson barking himself hoarse and the acoustics of all the hardwood floors, it was difficult to judge direction, but he was pretty sure the *bang* came from downstairs. And, thinking back, the screams had come from overhead.

Was that right?

Yes.

Miss Blackwell's shrieks had seemed to float above him on the summer breeze.

Which meant?

He was not keen on the idea of bursting into an elderly woman's bedroom. Talk about a great way to give someone a heart attack. Better to phone for help, right?

But she could easily have already had a heart attack or a stroke or a bad fall. In which case, time was of the essence.

Ellery reluctantly reached his decision. "Miss Blackwell? I'm coming up."

He waited a beat for a response, but still there was nothing. He ran up the stairs, pausing at the top.

He sincerely hoped she did not keep a hammer in her bedside table.

Or a gun.

"Miss Blackwell?"

Please don't let her be dead. He really, truly did not want to find another body, but concern, and *maybe* just a tiny bit of, yes, curiosity, drove him onward, down the shadowy hall with its cobwebs and peeling wallpaper.

The second level of the house was in a much worse state of disrepair than the ground level. It seemed Miss Blackwell's cleaning lady was not permitted on the upper level, which seemed, well, not odd exactly, but in keeping with what he knew of his eccentric customer.

He came to a room with a door slightly ajar. His heart began to pound faster. He pushed open the door, which moved on creaky hinges. He had a quick impression of high ceilings and bay windows with the blinds drawn, throwing the room into gloom.

"Miss Blackwell?" his voice came out huskily.

He was not expecting an answer, by then more than half convinced he was going to find her dead, so the faint moan that met his ears sent his heart ping-ponging around his chest.

His eyes strained the gloom, and he made out a long thin figure in a white nightdress lying facedown on the floor.

"Oh no."

From the porch below, Watson began to howl.

Ellery dropped to his knees beside her. "Can you hear me? Miss Blackwell?"

He found her wrist, felt for a pulse, and was relieved to feel a little flutter beneath his fingers.

He put his face close to what he could see of hers.

Her false eyelashes stirred, but her eyes remained closed. Beneath the heavy makeup, her face was bloodless, but he could see a bump forming on her temple. Her breath came out in little alcohol-scented gusts.

Not that Ellery didn't enjoy a few Bloody Marys over brunch with friends, but getting plastered by yourself at ten in the morning did not seem like a great idea. He wasn't judging, but this could explain—well, but could it really?

If she had fallen down the staircase, her screams might have made sense. But who screamed—who had *time* to scream—when they tripped and hit their head on a piece of furniture?

He scooted over to the bedside table and picked up the phone, listened, and was relieved to hear a dial tone.

Why?

He knew she had phone service. Had he imagined the phone line might be cut?

He dialed the island's emergency number and requested an ambulance.

Then he dialed Jack's cell.

After two rings, Jack's pleasant voice said crisply, "Chief Carson speaking."

"Jack," said Ellery with relief.

Jack's voice warmed noticeably. "Hey, you."

"Hey."

"What's up?"

"I don't know if it's anything. I might be over-reacting."

"Okay." Jack was cautious again.

"I'm at Juliet Blackwell's. I was delivering books. She's...well, I don't know what she is because she's unconscious."

"You need paramedics?" Jack was all business now. Ellery could hear the rustle of paper and the creak and shift of his leather chair.

"The ambulance is already on the way. The thing is, when I got here, she was screaming. She sounded scared out of her wits."

"I see." Clearly Jack did not, but he was doing his best.

"And I had the impression, but I could be wrong, that someone was in the house."

"Was she conscious when you found her? Did she say something to that effect?"

"No."

"Did you see—"

"I didn't see anyone or anything."

Ellery listened to their conversation through Jack's ears and winced. He should have just called PICO PD's emergency line and not bothered Jack with something like this. Like Jack didn't have enough on his plate?

Jack interrupted his uncomfortable reflections. "You want me to come and check things out?"

Honestly, Ellery had not thought that was even a possibility. Mostly he'd been hoping to hear Jack tell him why there was nothing to worry about and not to let his imagination run away with him.

"God. Could you? Or even if you sent someone else. I know how busy you are."

There was a hint of a smile in Jack's reassuring, "I'll be there in ten. Hang tight."

The call disconnected, and Ellery turned his attention to Miss Blackwell—and got another surprise. Her head was raised, her eyes open, and she was staring at Ellery, her gaze dark and confused.

"Hey, Miss Blackwell," he said gently. "How are you feeling?"

She said in a wondering tone, "Why, Ellery... it's you."

"Yep, it's me."

She made an effort to rise, and he scooted back and helped her turn over.

"I don't think you should try to get up yet. Everything's going to be okay. The ambulance is on the way."

"Ambulance…" Her eyes widened with alarm. "Oh, but I can't… I can't *leave*…"

Should he have called for the paramedics first and let them make the call on whether to transport her? He'd just assumed someone that old, that frail would have to go to the hospital to get checked out.

"You should probably hear what the paramedics have to say, right?"

"No. I don't care what they have to say. I can't leave." She tried to sit up and then sank back with a moan. She began to swear, and though Ellery was no prude, he was a little startled at the colorful stream of invective.

"I'm sorry," he said. "But you seemed to be out cold."

She broke off swearing and feebly patted his hand. "It's not your fault. You're a dear boy for trying to help."

"Do you remember what happened? Did you fall? Did you faint?"

She didn't reply. He wasn't sure she even heard his question. Her dark eyes stared past him so long, so intently, the hair rose on the back of his neck. He cast a quick look over his shoulder, half expecting to see someone standing in the doorway.

But no.

There was no one there.

And yet she was staring as though there *were* something there. Something both fascinating and terrifying.

Ellery asked softly, "Miss Blackwell?"

No response.

"Why did you scream?"

"He was here," she whispered, without looking away from whatever had captured her attention.

Ellery looked over his shoulder again, and this time he felt his scalp crawl as he realized that the long shadow in the corner of the room seemed to have a shape. Not a shadow. A silhouette. He could make out the tricorn hat, the long coat, the thin curving line of a sword.

Now that he saw it too, he couldn't seem to tear his gaze away.

Was it moving?

No.

Not a centimeter.

So what the heck was he looking at?

Could that really be—no. No way. Ghosts didn't appear in broad daylight. Fictional ghosts, anyway. And were there any other kind?

Come to think of it, there had been that ghost in *The Innocents*. That was pretty freaking terrifying.

But normally, no.

He tore his gaze from the unmoving silhouette, looked around the room, and saw that the body of the lamp on the table near the window was a tall bronze pirate figurine.

Relief made him sheepish.

Had he seriously thought— Had *she* seriously thought? No. She couldn't have. She'd lived in this house her entire life. She had to have noticed the shadows cast by the lamp before this morning.

"Who was here?" Ellery asked.

Miss Blackwell squeezed her eyes shut, as though in pain. She shook her head. "I was wrong."

"About what?"

"I was being s-silly. He couldn't be here. He's dead."

"Who's dead? Who did you think was here?"

She didn't answer.

Ellery said, "Okay. Just rest here. I'm going to grab the quilt from the bed—"

"*No.*" Miss Blackwell's hand shot out and gripped his arm, her scarlet nails digging into his forearm. "Don't leave me." Her eyes were black with terror.

"No, of course not," he said quickly. "I just thought you might be chilled, and the bed's right there…"

She shivered. "I'm not chilled."

The wail of an ambulance siren drifted in on the summer breeze, gaining volume as it drew near.

"That's the paramedics, Miss Blackwell. I have to open the door for them," Ellery told her. "I'll be right back. I promise."

Her false eyelashes lifted, and there was an odd gleam in her eyes. She stopped clenching his arm and smoothed her bony hand over his skin. "Yes. Tell them to go away. Then come back here."

Yeah. That was just not going to happen.

Ellery went downstairs, opened the door, and found the porch furniture completely rearranged by Watson, who'd managed to wrap his leash over the back of one chair, beneath the seat of another, and around the legs of a table. He had about a foot of leeway left in his leash, and he hopped with determination toward Ellery, inching the table forward.

"What in the..." There was no time to deal with the pup, however, as the ambulance had pulled in front of the house, lights flashing. The driver cut the siren.

Ellery went down the steps to meet them, giving them directions to Miss Blackwell's bedroom.

The paramedics rolled their gurney inside. Ellery trailed after, doing his best to stay out of their way.

Upstairs, Miss Blackwell assured them she was perfectly fine and did not require medical assistance, but it was a pretty feeble effort, and she was easily overruled.

Ellery watched as Miss Blackwell was carefully and efficiently lifted onto the gurney, strapped down, and rolled down the hall.

"This is so unnecessary," Miss Blackwell was still protesting as she was loaded into the ambulance.

One of the paramedics climbed in with her, the double doors were slammed shut, and away the ambulance went, dust flying, lights flashing.

Jack's white and blue police SUV passed the ambulance as it sped off down the road, siren keening through the still, hot air.

Ellery felt a little guilty, but he really didn't see what else he could have done. That bump on Miss Blackwell's head had to be checked out.

He waited as Jack parked, climbed out of his vehicle, and strode unhurried but purposeful across the ragged remnants of lawn. It was disconcerting the way his heart brightened whenever Jack appeared. But really, that wasn't only due to their relationship. There was something reassuringly calm and capable about Jack. When Jack was around, you just knew everything was under control.

"You okay?" Jack's boots sounded heavily on the wooden planks as he mounted the steps to the porch.

"Yeah. Fine. Thanks for coming, Jack."

"Of course." Jack brushed that aside, as though checking for prowlers was all part of the chief of police's daily routine. His brows rose as he observed the circle-the-wagons arrangement of porch furniture.

Watson tugged an ornate iron chair another few inches in his desperation to greet his beloved.

Ellery knelt to unfasten Watson from his leash. "Poor Miss Blackwell. She really didn't want to go to the hospital."

"Who does? Were you able to find out what happened?"

Watson, freed from the stranglehold, sprang up on his hind legs, whining for Jack's attention. Jack absently patted him hello, but this was not enough acknowledgment for Watson, who began to spring up and down.

"Watson, knock it off." Ellery answered Jack, "Not really. She regained consciousness, but I'm not sure she was totally herself. She said she thought someone was here."

Jack's blue-green gaze sharpened. "Did she say she was attacked?"

"No. She also didn't say she fainted or fell, though. There was a bump on her head."

"Okay. I'll have a look around."

"She did say it couldn't be the person she thought it might have been, because he's dead."

"Huh?"

"Miss Blackwell said something like, *He couldn't be here. He's dead.*"

Jack said gravely, "Uh-oh. That eliminates our prime suspect."

"Believe me, I know how it sounds."

"No. You did the right thing in calling." Jack stepped around Watson's impersonation of a pogo stick.

Ellery followed him to the door. "There's an open window in the kitchen, but that's where I came in. No one could have gone through before me because there would have been stuff smashed all over the floor. The wreckage is all mine."

"Okay."

Jack opened the door, started to go inside, paused as Ellery added, "When I walked into the foyer, I thought I heard a door slam, but I couldn't tell from which direction."

"Right. Let me take a look, and then I'll get your statement." There was the faintest of twinkles in Jack's eyes.

Ellery answered the twinkle. "Yes, I admit it. This place gives me the creeps."

Jack laughed. "Never fear, you've got your circus dog to keep you company." He went inside the house, closing the door behind him.

Ellery sighed and set about putting the porch furniture into some semblance of order. The house did make him uneasy, but he was also curious and would have liked to accompany Jack as he checked for intruders.

He opened the front door, dropped the bag of books inside, closed it again. Watson gave him a reproachful look, scratched half-heartedly on the front door a couple of times, and then wandered down the steps into what was left of the garden. Ellery walked to the edge of the porch to keep an eye on him.

It didn't take Jack long. The front door opened, and Jack stepped onto the porch and locked the door. He was holding a woman's black pocketbook as well as a ring of old-fashioned keys.

"I didn't even think about her keys or identification," Ellery said.

"I'll drop this stuff off at the hospital when I go interview her in a little bit." Jack studied him. "It doesn't look to me like anyone broke in. But that doesn't mean there wasn't an intruder. The side entrance door was open. The lock sticks."

"Open?"

Jack nodded.

"That's not good."

"No, it's not good. But the fact that someone could get in doesn't mean they did. Miss Blackwell's a very old lady. We don't know what medical conditions she might have. Even if she's in generally good health, she could have heard something, or imagined she heard something, jumped out of bed, got dizzy, and fell. She could have tripped and hit her head moving around in the dark."

True. Absolutely true. Except...it hadn't been dark. It had been midmorning.

"So this isn't a crime scene," Ellery said.

"I'll have to get Miss Blackwell's statement before I know what it is."

Ellery assented. Either way, he'd done his duty. "Thanks again for coming, Jack. I know it's the last thing you needed today."

"Any excuse to see Watson." Jack was grinning as he kissed Ellery—and then kissed him again.

His shoulder mic crackled into life. "Chief?"

Jack sighed. Responded, "Carson go."

"Are you coming back to base? We've got a situation here."

Jack looked skyward as though counting to ten. He said crisply, "10-19."

At the pronounced silence on the other end, he clarified, "Back to base."

"Right. I mean, 10-4!"

Jack shook his head. To Ellery, he said, "Hop in the SUV. I'll drop you off at the Crow's Nest."

CHAPTER FOUR

"You've had an eventful morning!" Nora greeted Ellery after Jack dropped him off at the Crow's Nest.

Ellery stared at her. "How could you already have heard about what happened? How is that even possible?"

"Bad news travels fast," Nora said cheerfully.

By now he shouldn't have been surprised at the efficiency and speed of the island's information superhighway.

Felix, squatting down to greet the ever-gregarious Watson, looked up at him. "Is Miss Blackwell going to be okay?"

"I hope so."

Felix nodded. He was twenty now, tall and willowy, with dark hair and blue eyes. His heart was set on an acting career, and with his looks and ability, he had a decent chance of achieving that dream. Or at least he had before the events at Skull House. Now... Felix seemed, to Ellery, a little lost.

"She was insisting she was fine when the para-medics carted her out of there. But she's got to be in her eighties. It looked to me like she'd hit her head on something."

"Or someone hit *her*," Nora said.

Ellery frowned. "*That's* how rumors get start-ed." He idly flipped open the remaining pastry box. Sadly, all that was left of the morning's pastries was one stale glazed doughnut.

Nora, not a bit chastened, replied, "Either way, it's the first time Juliet Blackwell has left her house in probably twenty years."

"Twenty *years*?" Felix and Ellery chorused.

Nora confirmed it.

No wonder the poor thing had been terrified.

Further discussion was cut short by the warning jangle of the front door. A large group of women and preteens filed in, soft drinks and ice-cream cones in hand.

Nora chirped, "Welcome to the Crow's Nest!"

The tweenagers got a good look at Felix and be-gan to giggle and whisper.

Ellery sighed for the health and welfare of his merchandise, retreated to his office, and got back to sorting through job applications.

So many job applications.

It was tempting to cull any applicant who didn't live on Buck Island, but the ferry ran year-round and a couple of the most qualified candidates were not local.

The salary he was offering for what was probably going to be part-time work might not even cover someone's transportation costs. But maybe that was a decision better left to prospective employees.

A rap on the doorframe of his office jarred him from his reflections. Felix hovered in the doorway, looking nervous. He was not by nature a nervous kid.

"Can I talk to you?"

Ellery said, "Sure. Have a seat. You can close the door if you want."

Felix closed the door and took the seat Libby had inhabited earlier. He drew a deep breath, said, "Is Libby okay?"

Ellery considered him thoughtfully. He liked Felix. He liked Libby. They were good kids, but they were still kids. He did not want to get involved in their problems.

"I don't know Libby well enough to know if she's okay," he said honestly.

Felix nodded, looked down at his hands gripping his knees.

Ellery said, "She's under a lot of stress right now. I know that much."

Felix nodded again.

"She could probably use a friend?"

Felix said bitterly, "Libby has plenty of friends. Everybody loves Libby."

Ellery understood that the bitterness was not directed at Libby. He felt for Felix. He really did. Especially since he felt to blame for a portion of Felix's misfortune. Felix was bearing some of the brunt of people's disappointment and anger toward his father. It wasn't fair. Life *wasn't* fair. That was one of the first lessons of adulthood. Only in kindergarten were cookies and stickers handed out in equal measure.

"Felix, I'm sorry. I know these last months haven't been easy. Once you're away at college, it'll be better."

Felix brushed that off. "It doesn't matter. I don't care what people think."

That was so obviously untrue, Ellery didn't bother replying.

"I just wondered about Libby. That's all." Felix rose.

"You could always ask her how she's doing." That was as far as Ellery was willing to go, and the minute the words were out, he wished he'd kept his mouth shut. He was always teasing Nora about meddling, and here he was, offering unsolicited advice on something he truly knew nothing about.

Felix's expression clearly communicated, *You, sir, are without a clue*, and he left the office.

Ellery mentally shook his head and returned to trying to set up interviews for the following day.

It had been an eventful first day back at work, and frankly, once six o'clock rolled around, Ellery would have liked nothing better than to head home, have a nice supper and a drink (his first in two weeks of convalescence) and spend a relaxing evening with Watson and a good book. But he'd promised Nora to look in on the Silver Sleuths book club, and apparently, he was acting as security consultant to Libby, so his dreams of a pleasant evening at home were going to go unfulfilled.

Before Nora departed for dinner, he headed over to the Salty Dog to check in with Libby.

Tuesday night or not, the pub was packed, and he could hear raucous laughter and the thump of a bass before he pushed open the door.

Smugglers drink of the Frenchman's wine,
And the darkest night is the smuggler's time,
Away we ran from the exciseman,
It's a smuggler's life for me,
It's a smuggler's life for me.

A few resigned-looking locals greeted Ellery as he worked his way through the crowd, but most of the faces were unfamiliar.

For months Ellery had been under the impression that the Salty Dog was Pirate Cove's only pub, but he'd recently learned that there was another less reputable pub called the Deep Dive. The Deep Dive was a locals-only hangout owned by the notorious Shandy family. During the summer months, more locals migrated to the tourist-free Deep Dive, but when the seasonal visitors cleared out, everyone headed back to the Salty Dog.

Ellery at last reached the bar, where an uncharacteristically harassed-looking Libby was pulling beers with the hasty precision of long practice. At nineteen, she was technically too young to be behind the stick, but Jack, ordinarily a stickler about such things, turned a blind eye to the Salty Dog's operations. That seemed to be one of the advantages of village life.

Spotting Ellery out of the corner of her eye, Libby topped off a mug and came to meet him. Her face was flushed and perspiring, reddish tendrils curling on her forehead.

"I was afraid you'd forget," she said.

"No, of course not."

Her smile was relieved. "I'll get you a key and the security-system code."

Ellery nodded, and Libby darted into the kitchen.

The Fish and Chippies launched into another rousing chorus:

Smugglers drink of the Frenchman's wine,

And the darkest night is the smuggler's time,

Away we ran from the exciseman,

It's a smuggler's life for me,

It's a smuggler's life for me.

Ellery listened absently, thinking again it was a pity the entrance to the tunnels beneath the village had been sealed off because that would have offered such a quick solution to Libby's—and his—problem.

Libby returned with a folded slip of paper and a ring of keys.

"How many guests are staying here now?" Ellery asked.

"Five. Two married couples, plus the adult daughter of the Owens. They're from New Mexico. The Klines are from New Jersey. With the exception of Pepper Owen, they're all returning guests. We've had them here several times over the years, and there's never been any problem."

"Okay. Thanks."

"Did you want to have dinner? On the house," she offered.

That was where he'd have to eat it too. There wasn't an empty seat in the place.

"That's okay. I've got a ton of work to catch up on."

"A hamburger for Watson?"

Watson would have been very disappointed to know Ellery turned that offer down. "That's okay. I've got a packet of his fancy-schmancy customized food in the mini fridge."

Libby nodded, smiled distractedly, and turned to deal with the next crisis.

"Just look at that suntan," marveled Mrs. Ferris a couple of hours later. "Ellery looks more like a movie star than ever!"

There were murmurs of agreement from the other members of the Silver Sleuths, with the exception of spry and acerbic Mr. Starling, who snorted in disgust at the very idea. He pumped Ellery's hand as if he'd just returned from a dangerous mission. "Good to have you back, my boy. The place isn't the same without you."

This too was met with unanimous consent.

Hermione Nelson, a heavyset woman in her late sixties with startlingly blue eyes and stiffly coiffed red hair, looked up from petting Watson (who was under the impression everyone was there to see *him*). "I agree. You're looking very well, Ellery. I think you needed a good rest."

"I'm sure he could have done without getting bashed over the head," Mr. Starling said.

Mrs. Nelson shrugged. Nora said breezily, "It's all part of the job, isn't it?"

Ellery gave her a look of disbelief. "What job am I supposed to have that getting knocked out is only to be expected?"

Mrs. Smith tittered. Mrs. Clarence, a sleek and stylish sixty-something, chuckled.

While the Silver Sleuths went about the all-important business of setting up the refreshments table, Ellery fielded questions about his health, as well as the morning's adventure at Miss Blackwell's. He was touched and a little surprised by the genuine-seeming warmth of the Silver Sleuths.

"Has anyone heard how Miss Blackwell is doing?" he asked.

No. No one had anything to report. Hopefully no news was good news.

In short order, the coffee urn was set up and plates of baked goods were circulating. In Ellery's opinion, the Silver Sleuths book club was really just a coffee klatch. Tea and cakes served with a generous dollop of gossip.

Not that there was anything wrong with that. Quite the contrary. The more established the Crow's Nest became as a village social center, the more their business seemed to grow.

"Did you hear about Sue Lewis?" Mrs. Smith said with a little sputter of cookie crumbs. She looked mortified and put a hand to her mouth.

"What about her?" If Ellery had a nemesis in Pirate's Cove, it would be the editor and owner of the *Scuttlebutt Weekly*. For reasons known only to herself, Sue had pretty much taken an instant dislike to him, and time and further acquaintance had only hardened her feelings.

"She, well, the paper, is up for the Our Town Award for Excellence in Community Journalism."

"Is that a real award?" Ellery wouldn't put it past Sue to make up her own award.

The others laughed.

"It's real," Mrs. Clarence assured him. "The competition is very stiff, though, so I don't know how much chance the *Scuttlebutt Weekly* has against places like Exeter and Foster."

The conversation moved on to various upcoming trials—a topic Ellery found uncomfortable in the extreme—and then, inevitably, the love lives of those not present. Dylan, it seemed, was still seeing new-comer September St. Simmons.

"That can't be the woman's real name," Mrs. Clarence said.

"It'll be a stage name," Mr. Starling said knowledgeably.

It was tricky when you didn't care for a close friend's boyfriend or girlfriend. Dylan Carter was probably Ellery's closest friend in Pirate's Cove, but he'd seen very little of him since Dylan had met September. Ellery didn't have anything against September, but she reminded him of a lot of people he'd known in the movie business. People with ambition where their hearts should be. He thought Dylan deserved better. And he missed him.

Granted, these days Ellery's free time was mostly spent with Jack, so maybe the feeling was mutual.

The big shocker of the evening was learning Janet Maples had been seeing Tom Tulley before he fell ill, and currently had the unlikely role of ministering angel.

Ellery couldn't help wondering if her father's new relationship with Janet was part of Libby's stress.

He was frowning over this idea when Nora announced, "We mustn't talk the evening away," and shooed everyone to the circle of chairs she and Ellery had set up earlier.

The Silver Sleuths carried their plates and cups to the circle of chairs and, on cue, pulled out battered copies of Diana Killian's *Corpse Pose*. The books seemed to bristle with sticky tabs and page markers.

Ellery eyed this performance skeptically. *"Really?"*

He was met by seven variations on the theme of polite surprise.

"Who do you guys think you're fooling? You're not still reading that book. I doubt if you've even started it."

"Oh..." Mrs. Smith looked confused. She looked to Mrs. Nelson, who pleasantly but determinedly attempted to stare down Ellery.

Ellery wasn't having any of it. He stared back. Mrs. Nelson was not to be outdone. She beetled her brows in disapproval. Ellery delivered the coup de grâce and arched one eyebrow.

Defeated, Mrs. Nelson slumped back in her chair.

Mr. Starling expelled a sigh of relief and tucked his copy back in his pocket. He rose and headed back to the refreshments table.

"If I wasn't here tonight, what, or should I say *whom,* would you be discussing?" Ellery asked.

"You, dear," Mrs. Nelson informed him.

Mrs. Smith giggled, and Nora threw her a look of exasperation.

"Well, since you can't talk about me—and there's nothing to talk about anyway—what's the story with Juliet Blackwell?" Ellery glanced at Nora. "I know there's a story. You've been dropping hints all day."

"*Clues*, dearie. There's a difference."

"Sure."

"You're certainly right about that," Mrs. Nelson said. "In her day, Juliet Blackwell was as notorious as they come."

"But you couldn't have known her in her day, Mrs. Nelson. You must be thirty years younger."

Mr. Starling gave a hoot of laughter. Mrs. Nelson ignored him, beamed at Ellery, and said to no one in particular, "This is why we love him."

Presumably she did not mean Mr. Starling.

Nora said, "You're right, dearie. Juliet is quite a bit older than the rest of us, but the Blackwell family used to play a prominent role in village affairs. I remember Juliet and her sister Cressida very well. They were always galloping their horses and racing their boats and speeding their sportscars all over the island."

"Juliet drove like a madwoman," Mr. Starling muttered.

Mrs. Nelson said, "They were like living, breathing advertisements for all the things visitors could do here on the island. They weren't only beautiful; they seemed so elegant and sophisticated compared to the rest of us. Every winter they went to New York to visit family, and they always came back with the latest and loveliest clothes."

"They were twins, weren't they?" Mrs. Ferris asked.

"No," Mr. Starling answered. "Juliet is two years younger. But they were always together. Two peas in a pod."

Mrs. Nelson said, "Juliet was the wild one. Cressida was more serious. The responsible one. Or so we all thought. After their mother died, Cressida took over her duties as hostess and mistress of the house, and when their father fell ill, she took that on as well."

"By then, they'd gone through most of the Blackwell fortune," Nora explained before Ellery could ask. "Not those two specifically, but the family as a whole."

"It was a lot to put on such a young woman," Mrs. Nelson said, "but Edgar Blackwell was of that generation."

What generation would that be? The indentured-servitude-isn't-so-bad generation?

"The old sod got more and more miserly and reclusive—"

Mrs. Nelson cut Mr. Starling off with a tart, "It's a family trait."

Nora said, "Juliet was engaged to be married to a wealthy young man she'd met the previous winter, and Edgar was determined that nothing should get in the way of that. Juliet was his favorite, but I'm sure he also expected his prospective son-in-law to bail him out. It didn't turn out like that."

"What happened?" Ellery asked.

Mrs. Ferris gave a harsh laugh. "Cressida ran off with her sister's fiancé."

"The dutiful, responsible one?"

"Not so dutiful and not so responsible, as it turns out."

"Yikes." Ellery turned to Nora. "So Cressida ran off to live the good life in New York, and Juliet was stuck looking after her ailing father?"

"Yes."

"That's pretty messed up. Did the runaway groom at least bail out his in-laws?"

"No. Well, he wasn't given the opportunity. Edgar disinherited Cressida."

"*Never darken my doorstep again!*" Mrs. Smith gave another of those breathy laughs.

"He was a little bit of an odd duck himself," Nora said.

"Edgar?"

"No. The fiancé. He was originally from Hungary, I believe. A self-made man."

Ellery said, "Not literally, one assumes. He must have had family."

"I suppose he did, but I seem to recall something about that. An estrangement?" Nora squinted at her long-ago memories, and shook her head. "It's so long ago."

"He'd have fit right in with the in-laws," Mrs. Nelson said. "I heard the old man ordered every photograph and painting of Cressida to be destroyed. And the few remaining servants were forbidden to speak her name."

Ellery was momentarily distracted. "Every painting? How many paintings of her could there be?"

"This was the twentieth century, dearie. Wealthy families still commissioned formal portraits to commemorate life's milestones."

"Right. I see. And was that the last of Cressida?"

"Yes. She seems to have accepted her banishment."

"Willingly, I imagine," Mrs. Clarence said.

"She did try to come back for the funeral," Mr. Starling said. "Juliet wouldn't have it."

"I don't blame her for being bitter," Mrs. Clarence said. "If the family fortune was gone, it was probably her last chance to snag a wealthy husband."

Mrs. Clarence had developed a taste for gothic romance in recent weeks.

"Poor Miss Blackwell," Ellery said. "I didn't realize she'd had such a sad life."

Nora made a noncommittal noise.

"They're an unlucky family," Mr. Starling said.

"Cursed," Mrs. Ferris said. "According to legend, anyway."

Nora said briskly, "More like the inevitable result of generations of bad decision-making. Edgar spoiled those girls. But Edgar's father spoiled *him*."

"That too," Mr. Starling agreed.

A funny silence fell. Watson, curled in a ball beneath Ellery's chair, began to snore. Pretty much the cutest sound in the world.

"Juliet could have escaped if she'd really wanted to," Mrs. Nelson said suddenly. "She could have sold the Black House after her father died. She could have moved anywhere she liked. It was her decision to stay."

"That's true," Mr. Starling put in. "Back then, the house and land would have fetched a pretty price. Instead, she parceled off most of the land in bits and pieces."

"The house would still fetch a pretty price," Mrs. Clarence said with the certainty of one who'd bought property on the island not that long ago. "Even in the shape it's presumably in."

The Silver Sleuths eyed Ellery inquiringly.

"It's not in terrible shape," he said. "And it's full of what look to me like genuine antiques. So yes, there's probably a decent amount of money tied up in the property."

"It's mortgaged to the hilt, I imagine," Mrs. Smith said.

"True." Mr. Starling brushed cookie crumbs off his paisley ascot. "But Buck Island property values have rocketed in the last decade. There could still be a lot of equity in the house and whatever acreage is left."

"Millions, I should think," Mrs. Clarence said.

Mrs. Nelson mused, "I wonder who inherits." She glanced at Ellery and added, "Eventually."

"Cressida's daughter, I imagine," Nora said.

The others looked surprised. "There's a niece?" someone asked.

"Yes," Nora replied. "In Newport, I believe. There may be other more distant relatives as well, but Edgar was always afraid people were after his money. I don't think he kept in close contact with extended family. I remember hearing him once call his own sister a *hanger-on*."

"What a lovely family," Ellery said.

"Who did the girls stay with in New York? Mrs. Smith asked.

"Their maternal grandmother. But she was gone by that time."

"Miss Blackwell never married, never had children of her own?" Ellery asked.

"No," Nora said slowly.

"That we know of," Mrs. Nelson said meaningfully.

Ellery could not interpret the looks the Silver Sleuths exchanged, but clearly there was more to this story than he'd yet heard.

Mr. Starling seemed to be answering those enigmatic looks when he said testily, "She never married that jackanapes!"

Ellery blinked. What in the heck was a *jackanapes*? It sounded politically incorrect in the extreme.

"Who knows what she did?" Mrs. Nelson argued. "It's not as though she'd have taken an announcement out in the paper."

Nora said, "I believe Stanley's correct. I don't think Juliet ever married the young man. Had she done so, she'd never have gotten rid of him so easily."

Ellery said, "I have zero idea what any of you are talking about."

From their expressions, he was pretty sure they'd forgotten he was listening in.

Nora said briskly, "Twenty years ago, Juliet had an affair with a young man who was vacationing on the island."

"A *very* young man," Mrs. Ferris said.

"How young?" Ellery asked.

"Felix's age," Nora said.

Not to be ageist, but twenty years ago, Miss Blackwell would have been in her sixties. That wasn't an age gap, it was an age chasm.

"What *was* his name..." mused Mrs. Ferris. "Robert? Roger? Something like that. Roger Mann. Was that it?"

"Robin, dear," Nora said. "Robin Mann."

Ellery asked, "I guess it didn't end well?"

Mrs. Nelson said, "None of her relationships ended well. He sneaked off like a thief in the night. It was after that, that Juliet locked herself away and became a hermit."

"Hermitess," Nora corrected.

Mrs. Nelson looked offended. "There's no such word."

"There certainly is," Mrs. Smith said.

"Then it's sexist."

Ellery intervened. "It's because of this failed love affair that Miss Blackwell locked herself away from the world?"

"*Exactly,*" the others chorused in relief.

"How long were they together?"

"About a year," Mrs. Nelson said.

"Less than a year," Nora objected. "No more than nine months."

Ellery said, "He could easily still be around. Is there any chance Miss Blackwell might have put him in her will? Assuming she has a will. Or would it all go to her sister? Or maybe the niece?"

"Oh, she has a will," Nora said with the certainty of one who had full access to the island hive mind.

"Where there's a will, there's a way," Mrs. Smith said lightly.

CHAPTER FIVE

He'd memorized the security code, but in the un-familiar after-hours dark of the Salty Dog's dining room, it took Ellery longer than he'd expected to find the alarm keypad. By the time he spotted the baleful blinking red light, he was bathed in sweat and dry-mouthed.

Any second the alarm was going to go off, and then what?

He punched in the numbers, watched tensely as the frantically flashing red light beat faster...and then turned green. He expelled a long, shaky breath.

He turned from the keypad and swung his flash-light on the silent room. Chairs were stacked on ta-bles, the floors had been mopped, the bar was shut-tered.

Nothing looked amiss.

He started for the kitchen, but Watson imme-diately got his leash tangled around one of the table legs. It took a minute to untangle him, because once Ellery knelt, Watson thought they were playing.

"No, Watson. *Down.*"

If a puppy's face could fall, Watson's face fell.

"Later. I promise," Ellery muttered.

It had been tempting to leave Watson napping comfortably in the car, but Watson could be very vocal when he was unhappy, and being left on his own was one of the things that made him most unhappy. The last thing Ellery wanted was to draw attention to his activities.

He got Watson calmed down and continued into the kitchen.

The double aluminum swinging door had just closed behind him when Ellery's cell phone began to vibrate, startling both him and Watson. Ellery fumbled for his phone as Watson began to bark, his shrill, indignant puppy voice bouncing off the hard floors and steel appliances.

Arf. Arf. Arf.

"*Shhhhh!*" Ellery did his best to hush Watson. "It's okay, buddy. It's okay. Really."

Watson was unconvinced, but subsided to muttering darkly beneath his breath.

Ellery pressed to accept the call and discovered to his chagrin that he was FaceTiming with his mother.

"Hi, you! Gosh, you're hard to get hold of these days!"

Ellery hastily reduced the volume on his phone. He half whispered, "Hi, Mom!"

"Do you have a cold? Your voice sounds funny."

Ellery cleared his throat. "Uh...a scratchy throat, yeah."

"Oh, baby. Summer colds are the worst."

Ellery's mother, Talia Alexander, was known for her roles in cerebral indie films like *Maiden Voyage, Shove,* and *Lost Summer.* Unlike Ellery, she was a very good actor. She was also very beautiful, with dark-brown hair and dark-brown eyes. Ellery loved her to pieces. She had a surprisingly deep laugh, stood a scant five feet in her stripey-stockinged feet, and was, per George, his stepdad, *a handful.*

Talia leaned forward, peering at the screen of her phone. "Where are you? You look like you're in a coal mine."

"Uh...nope. I'm in the kitchen."

"Why don't you turn on the lights? All I can see is the gleam of your eyes and your teeth."

"It's compli—" Inspiration struck. "We're having a power outage."

"Oh! Oh no. Poor you. Well, aside from no electricity and catching a cold, how are you doing? How's your little dog?"

Ellery turned his phone on Watson, who looked up and wagged his tail.

"Hi, cutie!" Talia called. "Oh my gosh, what a nose on that little guy. He's adorable."

"Sometimes," Ellery agreed.

"We keep missing each other. I feel like I haven't talked to you, really talked to you, in a year."

Ellery's gaze traveled over the shadowy racks of pots and pans, the industrial-sized fridge.

He said apologetically, "I know, and to be honest, this isn't a great time either."

"Oh, *Ellery*."

He winced.

"Ellery, you can't just fall off the face of the earth and think your dad and I are going to be okay with it."

Of all the times to have this conversation...

"Mom, come on. I didn't fall off the face of the earth. I'm in Rhode Island."

"*Exactly.* On an island in the middle of nowhere."

"It's not like it's a *deserted* island. I'm still getting settled, that's all."

"That's the part I don't understand. I thought the idea was to prepare everything for sale and then *sell* it. Why are you still *there*?"

"That was *not* my plan. My plan was to assess the situation and decide from there."

"You don't mean you're going to stay?"

"Yes, I do mean that."

"*Forever?*"

"For the foreseeable future."

"But what about your career?"

Ellery sighed.

"Baby, I'm serious!"

"I know you are."

"All right," Talia said briskly. "We won't argue about it. Yet. Your father and I are coming to see you next month. You can explain it to me then."

"Wait. *What?*" He hastily lowered his voice. "What did you say?"

"We're coming for a week. You don't have to worry about entertaining us or putting us up. We'll get a hotel."

"There are no hotel rooms this time of year. Everything is booked."

"We'll camp on the beach. We'll sleep on a park bench. Don't worry about it. I want to see you for myself and hear from your own mouth that you're happy and well and making the choices you want to make."

"Mom, I'm happy and well and making the choices I want to make."

"Great! But I want to see those choices for myself. Seriously, you could be a vampire for all I know."

"W-what?!" He remembered that he was standing in the dark kitchen at the Salty Dog, and laughed. "I think you'd know."

"I think I'd be the *last* to know. Anyway, we're coming, so no arguments. You're my only child. I have to know you're okay."

Ellery knew from long experience when he was beaten—which was pretty much every time he talked to his mother. But really, the truth was, he wasn't averse to her and George coming for a visit. He missed seeing her. He missed seeing George. This trip would probably be a lot of fun, although the timing felt awkward. Granted, that could have been present circumstances.

"All right, all right," he said. "Give me the dates once you have them, and I'll make sure I can take time off."

"No need. We don't want to be any bother," she said airily.

Ellery snorted.

"No, but seriously. You know us, we can amuse ourselves. So long as I can see for myself that you're okay."

"I know. You win. It'll be nice to see you guys."

"Likewise. Now go fix yourself a nice hot cup of turmeric ginger tea with a little honey and a splash of lemon. It'll do wonders for your throat."

"Sure," Ellery said.

"You're humoring me, but it really will help."

"I know."

"I love you. Your father loves you. Be good."

"Love you both—"

She clicked off in her usual decisive fashion.

Ellery shook his head, glanced at Watson watching him attentively. "Company's coming."

Watson wagged his tail.

Ellery pocketed his phone and turned his flashlight on the walls of the kitchen. He wanted to verify for himself that access to the tunnel system had truly been cut off.

It didn't take him long.

After poking around for a few minutes, he found the sealed-off area behind the commercial freezer. It looked like the opening had been boarded up and then plastered over. The plastered wall had never been painted over, making it easy to see the size and shape of the original doorway.

Everything was bone dry and hard to the touch. There was no possible way to get through without breaking down the wall.

So that was one theory—and frankly, the least likely—eliminated.

Ellery's second favorite theory, that the most likely culprit or culprits were pub guests, had taken a hit when Libby explained that the current guests were: A-middle-aged married couples, and B-returning guests. If the midnight crawler, er, prowler had only taken food or made a cameo appearance, it could have been chalked up to someone desperate for a midnight snack. But the fact that money and bottles of booze were disappearing changed the complexion of the case.

Ellery's *new* favorite theory was that the midnight prowler had to be a current or former employee of the Salty Dog. A former employee would know all the quirks and tics of Tom's security system, would probably even know the code to disarm the system, given how lackadaisical Tom's approach to security was.

Not that Ellery was criticizing that easygoing attitude. He was guilty of the same thing. He still didn't have a security system at Captain's Seat or the Crow's

Nest, despite his best intentions—and Jack's periodic reminders.

There was not a lot of employee turnover at the Salty Dog. Good jobs were hard to find on the island, and people tended to stay right where they were if they managed to land a decent placement. In the six months Ellery had been in Pirate's Cove, there had been no staff changes at the Salty Dog. Aside from Tom and Libby, there was Reg, the barman, and two waitresses, Carla and Frankie. Ellery didn't know any of them well, and hadn't formed any strong opinions about them. Reg had a heavier hand than Tom when building drinks. Carla flirted with all the male customers, be they six or sixty. Frankie had asked him for his autograph and often complained about her feet. They all seemed nice and pleasant and good at their jobs.

If an insider was to blame for the thefts, Ellery preferred to think it was a former employee rather than someone he knew and liked. But it was best to keep an open mind. You never knew what was going on with people behind the scenes. Everyone had stresses and strains in their life, and people handled pressure differently.

Which was why he couldn't rule out Libby, although she was definitely his least favorite suspect.

In fact, it was much easier to believe Libby was the target of these...pranks?...than the perpetrator. If the idea was to spook her, it was definitely working. Which was why he was willing to spend a good portion of his night in the empty pub, waiting and watching.

Not that he really expected anything to happen.

According to Libby, the midnight prowler had struck at least three times, but not consecutively and never on the same night. Never on the weekends either, which made sense. The pub was open later on weekends, and there was a lot more foot traffic to contend with, especially during the summer.

So Ellery figured he had a one-in-five chance that tonight might be the night.

Even if it wasn't, this gave him a chance to see for himself what the setup really was and whether it would be possible for someone to sneak downstairs.

He settled in a chair in a corner near the fireplace, close to where he'd often eaten during the winter and spring. Watson curled into a tight little ball, tucked his nose beneath his tail with the air of an old man pulling on his nightcap, and went to sleep.

The moon moved across the sky, the shadows lengthened.

Ellery thought about his mother's phone call. He was genuinely looking forward to the visit. But he was a little uncertain about Jack meeting his parents. Not that he didn't want them to meet—he most definitely did—but he didn't want any pressure on their relationship.

The best thing was to maybe sound out Jack, and if Jack seemed at all uncomfortable, Ellery would drop the idea of introducing him to his parents.

The minutes ticked slowly by.

Once upon a time, Ellery had been a night owl. There was a reason New York was known as the city that never sleeps. Half the time, his evenings hadn't really revved up until ten o'clock or so. Since moving to the island, Ellery had changed from night owl to early bird, and an hour into his impromptu stakeout, he realized he was in danger of dozing off.

He took out his phone, checked for any messages from Jack. He didn't expect to find a spur-of-the-moment invitation, which was good because there wasn't one. Jack was very clear about whether he would call or not, whether they would get together or not, and he rarely deviated from plan.

To keep from falling asleep, Ellery played a few rounds of Scrabble GO, competing against the app itself in Expert mode.

He liked games, and he enjoyed competition, but his favorite thing about Scrabble in all its forms was that it gave him the opportunity to work through his problems without consciously working through his problems. Sorting through a jumble of letters, trying to make sense of random vowels and consonants, turned out to be a great way of subconsciously sifting through his concerns and anxieties.

There had been a time, and not so long ago, when he'd Scrabbled at meal times, Scrabbled in the bath, Scrabbled before bed, Scrabbled during any stretch of time not taken up by physical activity. But now he had Watson. He had Monday game nights with Dylan and other friends. He had Nora. And he had Jack.

Sadly, Jack's name showed up in Ellery's Scrabble rack more than the real Jack showed up in Ellery's, er, rack—and tonight was no different. Also in Ellery's rack: cold, storage, yo, ho, trickery, blackheart, bacon, moxie, unforgiving, propensity... In other words, the usual. Once upon a time, he'd have drawn words like *audition, Broadway, options, clause, reboot.*

He continued to play, absently listening to the joints and joists of the pub get comfortable.

Outside the diamond-paned windows, the streets of Pirate's Cove grew darker and quieter...

He didn't realize he was asleep until the alarm went off.

The clamor was DEAFENING. It sounded like every pot and pan in the pub was being banged repeatedly with hammers. Ellery was on his feet before he was fully awake, and just managed not to fall over Watson who, adding to the cacophony, was barking furiously.

Over the disorienting din, Ellery heard a woman's outraged, *"They turned on the alarm?"*

He dropped his phone, hearing the forbidding *clunk* as it hit the floor, fumbled for his flashlight, and turned it in the direction of the door. It took a moment to make sense of what he was seeing. A slight figure in drab olive shorts, safari jacket, and bucket hat stared at him through night goggles.

Goggle being especially apt, given their mutual-
ly shocked expressions.

"Who are *you*?" she demanded.

"Who are *you*?" Ellery retorted, although he
already had a very good idea of who she had to be.
"Why are you dressed like that?"

"Pepper Owen. I'm a birder and I have mace."
She drew out a canister of something that did look
alarmingly like it could be mace.

Ellery had started toward the alarm, but he reversed course at that news.

"Don't mace me. I'm supposed to be here."

"What?"

He shouted—and it sounded even nuttier the second time, "Don't mace me. I'm supposed to be here."

She shouted back, "You're *supposed* to be here?
What does that mean? You must be crazy."

Yes. Indeed, he must.

Ellery put his hands up. "I'm going to turn off
the alarm. Don't mace me. Please."

Lights, blinking on in the hall above them, illuminated the forest of stacked tables and chairs. Voices, thick with sleep and high alarm, were calling out
for answers.

"What's happening?"

"Is the building on fire?"

"I think the building is on fire!"

"Where's Pepper? Is she back?"

Watson, as though having reached his breaking point, began to howl.

Really, it was hard to imagine how the situation could get any worse, barring the building actually catching fire.

Ellery crossed to the alarm, punched in the code, and the deafening racket cut off as though he'd yanked the plug. Only Watson continued to howl, sounding tiny and forlorn in that sudden silence.

It wasn't silent for long.

Pepper cried, "A bed check? Really? What kind of hotel sets a curfew for their guests? I'm forty years old! I'm not going to be dictated to. Nobody tells me when I have to go to bed. How dare they?"

Not that she didn't have a point, but she was still wearing her hat and night goggles, and the picture she presented was pretty disconcerting. Ellery tried to answer, but he was drowned out by the four irate, gray-haired, bathrobe-clad guests on the second landing, who were all talking at once.

"Is she all right?"

"Is the fire out? How did a dog get in here?"

"Pepper, honey, are you all right?"

"I don't think there was a fire, folks. I don't smell smoke. Pepper, is there a dog with you? Do you see flames?"

"I'm fine!" Pepper called. "We need to cancel our reservation. The management has someone doing bed checks!"

Ellery tried again. "Really, this isn't a bed check—"

"Then what are you doing sitting here in the dark waiting for me?"

Question for the ages.

Ellery tried a different approach. "You must have known about the curfew when you booked your room."

"*I* didn't book these rooms. You couldn't *pay* me to stay here!"

"Okay, but you knew the rules once you checked in. There's no one on the premises at night, so they have to lock the doors at midnight."

"That's ridiculous! This is the twenty-first century! They need to get key cards like a real hotel."

Yes, Tom did. But that would take money, and Tom was no more eager to spend money he didn't have to than the next business owner. Especially since the Salty Dog only rented rooms June through August.

Anyway, Ellery had no intention of arguing with her—especially when she was right—nor was he about to tackle the indignant customers on the second floor. It was painfully clear that any chance of surprising the midnight prowler had evaporated. Certainly for that night, and maybe for good, if the guests at the Salty Dog talked publicly about their experiences, and why wouldn't they?

"Okay. Sorry for the misunderstanding—"

"*Misunderstanding?* The only misunderstanding here—"

Across the room, his phone began to vibrate. Ellery snatched it up, saw that the caller was Libby. She was probably watching the entire scene play out on CCTV. He prayed he was about to be fired.

CHAPTER SIX

A persistent and annoying buzz infiltrated Ellery's dreams, ruining a perfectly enjoyable dream about birdwatching with Jack.

Was it already time to wake up? Couldn't be. It was still dark outside. Hadn't he just fallen into bed?

He shifted, feeling for his phone and dislodging Watson, who moaned and tried to snuggle closer. It was such a human sound and such a human response that it always made Ellery laugh, even when he was still half-asleep. *Ah.* There it was. He spotted his phone, illuminated and blinking in the gloom, buzzing incessantly.

The only person he could think of who would call at this hour was Jack, so he swiped the screen to answer without bothering to check the number.

"Hello?"

One of these days he'd learn to look before he leaped.

"Ellery, my dear?"

He'd gone to bed thinking of his parents' up-coming visit, so for a split second he thought that soft voice was his mother's. Happily, the cobwebs cleared before he addressed his caller as *Mom*.

How on earth had Miss Blackwell got his cell-phone number? It wasn't a number he gave out casually, so his confusion was probably obvious as he replied, "Miss Blackwell? How are you feeling?"

"Quite well, dear." Miss Blackwell's voice was uncharacteristically muted and vague. "The doctors say I might be able to leave in a few days."

"That's great. I'm glad to hear it." He was, of course, but he was also perplexed as to why he was getting this update at... He squinted at his phone's screen. Five forty-five in the morning. He was sympathetic, though, because he knew exactly how it felt to wake up in a hospital and be unable to sleep.

It was a wonder that anyone ever *did* sleep in a hospital.

"Thank you, dear. I know it's early, but...but I must speak to you right away."

"Oh?" Ellery asked uneasily. "Okay."

There was a weird pause.

"I'm listening," said Ellery.

"Not on the phone, dear. Could you drop by the hospital sometime today? Preferably as soon as possible?"

"Um...well, I can try." Ellery mentally ran through the day's schedule, which as far as he knew would be spent reading résumés and conducting interviews. He said reluctantly, "I could probably drop by after lunch."

"I know how busy you are, and I don't mean to press, but..." She fluttered on, pressing and then apologizing for pressing.

She's old. She's alone. It's a few minutes out of your life.

"You know what," Ellery interrupted. "Why don't I drop by about ten this morning? I've got a couple of prospective employee interviews, but I could squeeze in a visit after that."

"That would be *so* lovely."

After a few more pleasantries, Ellery ended the call. He glanced at Watson, who was giving him the side-eye.

"*You* try saying no to her."

Watson reserved comment, rolled onto his back, and prepared for his morning tummy rub.

Ellery arrived at the Crow's Nest before Nora, having found it impossible to fall back asleep after Miss Blackwell's phone call.

Well, and the flood of memories of the previous night's catastrophe.

His hopes (by then prayers) that Libby would fire him, had gone unanswered. Probably because Libby didn't believe she had any other options.

"At least we're making progress," she'd told Ellery after smoothing the ruffled feathers of her understandably irate guests.

"I don't think you could call this progress," Ellery had objected.

"But it is. You're eliminating suspects."

"Am I, though?"

Libby misunderstood. "Yeah, the birdwatching at four o'clock in the morning *is* pretty suspicious."

"I don't know if it is or not, but once tonight's fiasco gets out, I can't imagine your prowler will be back."

Libby did not seem as reassured by that as he'd hoped, and she had certainly shown no sign of letting him off the hook. Between Libby's misplaced faith and Miss Blackwell's mysterious summons, no wonder he had trouble falling back asleep.

He was sorting through more job applications—they kept flooding in—when Nora arrived about a half an hour later. He filled her in on his adventures at the Salty Dog, which she seemed to find highly amusing.

After that, they went over the applications he had selected for possible interviews, and by then, it was time for coffee with Jack.

On mornings when Jack and Ellery didn't wake up together, Jack usually stopped by the Crow's Nest for coffee, as he had done back before they were dating.

Right on time, the bell on the door chimed a silvery welcome, and Jack walked in carrying two tall cups of coffee. A ray of sunshine in navy blue poly-cotton blend.

"Sorry. They were out of oat creamer," he warned.

"*Out?* At eight thirty in the morning?"

"They've been out since yesterday, per the barista."

"Thanks, I needed this." He gratefully accepted the coffee cup Jack handed to him.

Jack did not kiss him—and Ellery did not expect him to.

Though they weren't hiding their relationship in any way, Jack rarely greeted Ellery in public as anything more than a friend. He did not go in for PDAs, which Ellery understood. Police Chief was kind of a tricky role. Finding the perfect balance between being approachable and responsive yet appearing always prepared to enforce the law was not easy.

Jack bumped Ellery's coffee cup with his own. "Cheers."

Ellery sipped his coffee. "Mm. And people say you can never find a cop when you need one."

Jack was amused. "Rough night?" He'd probably be less amused when he learned what Ellery had actually been up to the previous evening. Ellery was holding off explaining about that until they were somewhere they wouldn't be interrupted.

"You'd be surprised. How was dinner with the town council?"

Jack, who had knelt to greet Watson, rose. "Hard on the digestion. Nan is insisting that a special election be held in the fall."

Assistant Mayor Nan Sweeny, Nora's niece, had had to assume the role of mayor when Cyrus Jones had been forced to step down.

"You can't blame her. She's got her own business to run, and this is her busiest time of year too."

"I know. It's just that she's such a good mayor."

"Well, maybe the next mayor—"

Jack said grimly, "George Lansing plans on running."

"*Your* George Lansing?"

"Not mine. Definitely not mine."

Lansing was a detective, officially, the only detective, with PCPD.

"I thought he was bucking for your job," Ellery commented.

That was something Jack had confided the first night he and Ellery had spent together at Captain's Seat. Jack had not seemed at all worried; he had simply wanted Ellery to understand why Lansing had been such a hard-ass in the Brandon Abbott investigation.

Jack grimaced. "Turns out, he's setting his sights higher." He shrugged. "Anyway. We still on for tonight?"

"Dinner at my place?"

"Sounds like the best part of my day."

Ellery dropped an eyelid in a broad and playful wink. "And, hopefully, *night*."

Jack chuckled a little evilly, and said to a point just past Ellery's shoulder, "Morning, Nora."

Ellery jumped, turned, and got a good look at Nora's beaming countenance.

"Nora, I'm going to tie a bell around your neck."

"Better than a noose," she returned cheerfully.

Jack said, "The day is young." He surprised Ellery with a quick, light peck on the mouth, said, "See you about six," and departed.

The bell on the door jingle-jangled, then fell silent.

Ellery's first interview of the day was with a pretty high-schooler by the name of Addison Something. Addison brought her report card, which indicated she had received straight A's the previous semester. Ellery read it dutifully and handed it back.

"Congratulations." He'd never received straight A's in his life, so he was sort of impressed and sort of puzzled as to why she thought her report card was relevant.

"Thank you."

"Okay, so tell me why you'd like to work at the Crow's Nest."

Addison sat up straighter in her chair. "My mom says I have to get a job or she'll take away my car."

You had to give her points for honesty, right? He said, "I see. Basically, you don't care what the job is, you just need a job."

"Exactly," she said eagerly.

"Have you ever worked in a bookstore before?"

"No." She looked regretful.

"Do you love books? Do you like mysteries?"

Addison looked doubtful. "I can read, if that's what you mean." She held up her report card as a reminder.

No. That was not even close to what he meant.

GET THE HOOK!

Ellery's second interview of the morning was with Betty Ewing. Betty was middle-aged and wore a pink cat T-shirt with sequins, cat earrings, and cat-shaped eyeglasses. Still, Watson was not doing the hiring, and Ellery wanted to give her a fair chance.

"Betty, I see you've been out of the workforce for several years—"

"It's true. I was in Gloria McDonald Women's Facility."

Ellery said cautiously, "I see. Is that a correctional facility?"

"Yes."

He was wondering if he was allowed to ask her what she'd been in for—he'd never had to interview anyone for anything before now—when she volunteered, "Assault with a deadly weapon. But it was all a misunderstanding."

"Right. Of course," Ellery said quickly. "Betty, what makes you think you're a good fit for this job?"

"Well, I'm great with animals."

"That's nice, but—"

"I *love* animals."

"Sure, but—"

"Animals are *so* much nicer than people."

NEXT!

Ellery's third and final interview of the morning was with the unfortunately named Dick Dix. The good news was Dick was already gainfully employed on the island at Macao Trading Company, which sold T-shirts and souvenirs.

"Why do you want to leave MTC?" Ellery asked.

Dick, bald, grizzled, and nearly busting out of his red Hawaiian shirt, snarled, "I can't stand that bleeping bunch of idiots another minute!"

So yeah, that was the bad news.

Dick went on to share everything he hated about working at MTC, and then detailed what he disliked about each of his coworkers, his boss, and all their customers.

By the end of that diatribe, Ellery was feeling a little dazed. Out of morbid curiosity, he asked, "Where do you see yourself in five years?"

Dick waved to the office door. "Out there on the beach."

NEXT!

So that was that.

"It's early days," Nora comforted when Ellery rejoined her at the front desk. "And we still have..."

"Seventy," Ellery informed her gloomily. "Seventy more possible candidates."

"There's bound to be someone in there who's right for us."

"Libby's working full-time at the Salty Dog. Felix will be gone at the end of August."

"Plenty of time," Nora assured him.

Felix, busy reshelving, said, "You could run a more targeted want ad in the *Scuttlebutt Weekly.*"

"I wouldn't run an ad with Sue Lewis if she was the last newspaper in town."

"She *is* the last newspaper in town," Nora said.

Ellery groaned.

From behind the bookshelf, Felix mimicked, "*Well, I'm great with animals!*"

Nora and Ellery looked at each other and started laughing.

CHAPTER SEVEN

Shortly before ten, Ellery strode into the reception area of the island med center, holding a freshly purchased bouquet of yellow carnations. After asking for Miss Blackwell at the front desk, he was directed down a long hall redolent of antiseptic and cleaning fluids.

Miss Blackwell had one of the only private rooms in the center, so her family fortunes might have fallen, but they couldn't be completely depleted. When Ellery arrived at her door, he found it closed. From inside, he heard raised voices.

Or rather, one raised voice.

He listened for a moment. That soft, fretful murmur was Miss Blackwell. The other voice, also female, was louder, insistent, and only too familiar.

How the heck had Sue Lewis got in to see Miss Blackwell? It sure didn't sound like it had been Miss Blackwell's idea.

Ellery opened the door.

Sue, trim and tailored, as if preparing to anchor the national evening news, stood at the foot of Miss Blackwell's hospital bed. Miss Blackwell sat bolt upright, clutching the bedclothes to her chest.

"How dare you?" she quavered. "Get out of my room!"

Probably nothing Sue hadn't heard a million times before, and she was not impressed.

"Sooner or later, the truth always comes out, Miss Blackwell. It's better to get ahead of the story than be overtaken by events you can't control. Believe me, you want the press to be on your side. Otherwise—"

Ellery said, "Here's some hard-hitting journalism in action. Sue, do you think you could maybe wait until she's discharged from the hospital?"

Sue jumped guiltily and turned. "Well, well. Ellery Page. In the flesh."

"Not so far. If I thought it would get rid of you..."

Sue's flushed face turned ever redder. "That's called sexual harassment!"

Ellery just managed not to roll his eyes. "Come off it, Sue."

Ever since Ellery had had it out with Sue at the office of the *Scuttlebutt Weekly*, he'd felt a delightful indifference to anything she thought, said, or printed in her newspaper. Which didn't change the fact that Sue did still own and manage the village's only real communication platform. That power was something she was well aware of.

"No, *you* come off it. And if you *dare* threaten me again—"

"*Threaten* you? Really?"

"Yes, really!"

Ellery noticed Miss Blackwell frantically pressing the nurse call button. He couldn't blame her. His interruption hadn't exactly helped matters.

He said evenly, "You know what I think? You're attacking me because you're guilty about something. I wonder what. Harassing little old ladies in their hospital beds?"

"Me attack *you*! How ironic."

"How did you get in here? Who gave you permission to interview Miss Blackwell?"

"*She* did."

Miss Blackwell looked outraged. "I never!"

"Yes, you did." Sue was smiling a tight little smile. "I asked if you were allowed visitors, and you said yes."

Miss Blackwell began to sputter.

At that moment, two nurses in powder-blue scrubs entered the room. Ellery recognized Daisy from his own recent hospital stay. The older nurse, who was unknown to him, said in severe tones, "I'd like to remind both of you that this is a hospital, not a war zone. Your voices can be heard down the hall."

"Sorry," Ellery apologized.

"It's too late for sorry. I'll have to ask both of you to leave this instant."

"Cool your jets," said Sue. "I was leaving anyway." However, she just couldn't resist a parting shot at Ellery. "For your information, I'm a bona fide investigative reporter. I don't just sit around reading Agatha Christie all day and pretending that qualifies me to investigate crimes."

"I run a bookstore. I don't sit around reading all d—"

"You're not the only one in this village who can stumble over the solution to a mystery!"

Ellery opened his mouth, closed it, said mildly, "I'm not going to touch that one."

Sue heard the mental replay, turned still another shade of crimson, and turned her back to him. She told Miss Blackwell, "We'll talk again, Miss Blackwell."

"No, we won't," Miss Blackwell called back as Sue stalked out of the room. She impatiently waved off Daisy as she tried to take her vitals. "Not now. Not now."

When the older nurse turned her death-ray gaze on Ellery, Miss Blackwell intervened.

"Not him. He can stay. I asked him to come here."

"Dr. Mane—"

Miss Blackwell said firmly, "Ellery is family."

Ellery threw her a quick look but didn't argue. Daisy murmured she would get a vase for the flowers. He let her take the bundle of carnations.

Miss Blackwell said impatiently, "Never mind all that. Get out, both of you."

Daisy and the other nurse exchanged glances, and without another word, left the room, closing the door firmly behind them.

All the energy seemed to drain out of Miss Blackwell. She closed her eyes, said, "What a dreadful woman."

"I can't say I'm a fan."

Miss Blackwell's eyes popped open. "I can't imagine what story she thinks she's pursuing." There was a speculative gleam in her gaze. "She certainly hasn't treated you very fairly in her columns."

Ellery shrugged. "She's no fan of mine either. But I don't think you have to worry about her sneaking in here again. The hospital staff will be watching for her."

"I hope you're right." Miss Blackwell shook her head. "I admire a woman with ambition and guts. A woman should never be afraid to go after what she wants. But *she's* just rude. I'll never willingly speak to her."

"Anyway," Ellery said cheerfully, "I'm glad to see you looking so much better."

The shrill laugh that escaped Miss Blackwell surprised him. "I'm afraid that isn't much!"

"Well…" So much for diplomacy. Ellery dragged the chair to the bed and sat down. "How are you getting along?"

Miss Blackwell held her hand out, and he clasped it, feeling a little uncomfortable when she continued to hold on to him, gazing into his eyes.

"Thank you for coming. It means everything," she whispered.

"I'm glad I was able to." He studied her pale, bruised face. Without her usual makeup and false eyelashes, she looked naked, defenseless.

"And you even brought me my favorite flowers."

"Are they?" Ellery said. "I thought they were nice and cheerful."

"Of course, I would like any flowers *you* brought me."

Ellery smiled politely. He couldn't help asking, "What was Sue alluding to with that *the truth will out* stuff?"

"Who knows."

The way Sue's mind worked, she probably thought Miss Blackwell was trying to pull some kind of insurance scam. Sue was one of those naturally suspicious people. She still seemed to believe Ellery was a murderer waiting to happen.

Ellery said, "You talked to Chief Carson about everything that happened yesterday, right?"

Was it only yesterday? It felt like weeks had passed since he'd discovered Miss Blackwell lying unconscious in her bedroom.

She perked up a little. "Oh yes. Of course. He's a wonderful man. Very patient with a confused old lady."

Ellery smiled, but one thing Miss Blackwell had never seemed to him was confused. She didn't seem confused now either. She did seem, well, sort of evasive.

He asked kindly, "Do you remember much about what happened yesterday? I'm sure it was a frightening experience."

"Yes. Yes it was. But that's why I felt I had to speak to you right away. Chief Carson said something that led me to believe I might have given you the wrong impression."

"Like what?"

"That I saw someone."

"Well…"

She was watching him very closely. "Someone I-I *knew*."

"Not exactly," Ellery said. "You did say, *He was here*, but then you said something like, *It couldn't be him, he's dead*."

Miss Blackwell's fingers clenched around Ellery's, but she gave another of those unnerving, shrill laughs. "I suppose that would…would cloud the issue. But I never said his name, did I?"

"No."

"No." Her eyes had a funny glitter. "After all, it's true. Quite true. He *is* dead. He's been dead for nearly three hundred years."

Ellery gently freed himself. "You think you saw the ghost of Rufus Blackwell?"

"Yes." That was unequivocal enough.

Ellery frowned. "Do you mean you saw someone dressed up like Rufus Blackwell, or do you believe you actually saw a ghost?" Frankly, either seemed like a stretch.

"I hope you won't laugh at me."

He seemed to have gained an unfortunate reputation for laughing at inappropriate times. "No, no. I won't laugh."

"I saw the ghost of Rufus Blackwell. It's not the first time."

"It's *not*?"

"No. He—it—appeared at midnight for three nights before my father died."

"Oh?"

"I only saw it once. My father saw all three apparitions—and then he was dead."

"That must have been pretty...alarming."

As much as Ellery liked to think he kept an open mind, he was skeptical of this whole ghost business. After all, his entire film career had been centered on spooky manifestations that looked realer than real. Lights, cameras, and imagination (especially imagination) could create illusions capable of fooling almost anyone.

Miss Blackwell was watching him with her dark, unfathomable gaze. "The first time I saw the ghost, I wanted to believe it was a coincidence. There's a family legend, you see."

OF COURSE THERE WAS.

Ellery made a noncommittal sound.

"My grandmother always claimed she saw the ghost before my grandfather's death, but being young and naive, I never believed it. Until my own father's death. And even then, I think perhaps I still clung to a shred of doubt." She shook her head. "No longer."

Ellery digested this for a moment, asked cautiously, "Do you believe the ghost of Rufus Blackwell appeared to you for some particular reason?"

"Perhaps. I hope not. I hope I'm wrong." Before Ellery could respond, she said briskly, "But you see, that's why I wanted to clear up any misunderstanding. There was no intruder in my home. I don't want—I don't need the police hanging around, poking into things that are none of their business."

"Right. Okay."

"I don't mean to sound ungrateful. But I like my privacy."

"Of course," Ellery said. "I understand. I'm sorry I called Chief Carson. I had the impression someone else was in the house, which is probably why I misunderstood what you were saying."

"No, no," she said, reaching for his hand again. "You're not to blame. It means so much that you were looking after my best interests. You're always welcome in my home."

"Thank you."

"The truth is, I had lain down for a little nap. I was dreaming, and I thought I heard a noise. I got out of bed too quickly, fell, and hit my head on the nightstand."

Her account neatly matched Jack's theory. Was that actually what happened? If so, where did the ghostly sighting come in? Had she seen Rufus Blackwell in her dreams?

He was going to ask when she had seen the ghost, but she said, "Thank heavens you came when you did."

"Yes. I'm glad I was able to be of help."

"I wonder if I could further impose on your kindness?"

"Of course," Ellery spoke automatically, ignoring that sinking feeling.

"That fool of a doctor intends to hold me here for another day or so. Would it be too much of a favor to ask you to get the books you left at my house and bring them here?"

He said kindly, "Yes, I could do that."

She beamed. "That would be wonderful. Hospitals are so depressing. I don't have anyone to talk to, and I don't care to watch television."

She let go of him, pointing at the nightstand. "My keys are in there."

He opened the drawer and took out her keys.

"If you could just pick up my books and bring them here." She smiled. "It gives me another chance to see you."

Ellery smiled weakly.

"And if you could make sure that everything is still locked and secure. Now that word is out that the house is empty, I'm afraid some of these young hooligans might try to break in."

"I know Chief Carson locked everything up, but I'm happy to take a look around."

"Marvelous. Thank you."

"If you like, I can let the chief know you'd like an officer to stop by each night and take a look around? Just to make sure everything is okay."

"Oh no," she said. "I don't need anything like that. Just have a quick look around and then bring my books to me."

"Sure," Ellery said. How could he refuse? She was old and hurt and lonely. It wasn't much to ask.

"Thank you, Ellery. You're such a dear boy."

Maybe yes. Maybe no. A confused boy, certainly. One minute Miss Blackwell was dismissing the idea of intruders, the next she was sending him to make sure no one had broken into her house.

What exactly was she afraid of?

CHAPTER EIGHT

Ellery softly closed the door to Miss Blackwell's hospital room and headed toward the clearly marked exit.

"I'd recognize those stitches anywhere," said a voice behind him.

Ellery glanced around in surprise and met the smiley green eyes of Dr. Mane.

Ellery grinned back. "I get compliments everywhere."

"I bet you do." Before Ellery could react, Mane added, "Visiting Miss Blackwell, I presume?"

"I was. And I wasn't the only one. Sue Lewis, the editor of the *Scuttlebutt Weekly*, was in before me. I think she upset Miss Blackwell."

"So I heard." Mane said with unexpected steel in his tone, "Don't worry. There won't be a repeat performance."

Mane was a little older than Ellery. Tall, well-built, with curly blond hair and chiseled features. He looked a bit like Ellery's ex, Todd, but Ellery did not hold that against him.

"How soon do you think before Miss Blackwell will be released?"

Mane raised his eyebrows, and Ellery wondered if that was an inappropriate question from a non-family member. But then Mane relented, "I'd like to hold her a few days. She has a bump on the head, though no concussion, and there's a minor dislocation of the phalange."

At Ellery's blank look, Mane held up his hand, wiggled his little finger in greeting, and said, "That would be the bones of the pinky."

"Oh, right. So nothing too serious?"

"Nothing too serious, but falls are no joke at her age. Plus, she hasn't seen a doctor in over twenty years. I think she could do with a thorough checkup."

"Right." Ellery had no doubt that was true.

"However, she's dead set on getting out of here as soon as possible, so who knows."

"I remember the feeling."

Mane said, "Yes. It must be my cooking."

Ellery laughed. Mane's kooky sense of humor appealed to him. You didn't really expect a doctor to be funny. Come to think of it, was that even advisable?

Mane said with sudden casualness, "Anyway, sorry I wasn't here to clear you for takeoff yesterday, but according to Nurse Jay, you're feeling back to one hundred percent."

"I feel great. And I appreciate all the care I received."

"That's what we're here for."

There were some people you just instantly liked, felt an instant rapport with, and that was how Ellery felt about Dr. Mane.

They smiled at each other for a moment, and then Mane said, "I guess you're here working on a case?"

"A case?"

"You're a-an amateur sleuth, right?"

"That's...debatable. It's definitely not my job description. I run the Crow's Nest."

"The island's only mystery bookstore," Mane agreed.

"That's right."

"I'm going to have to broaden my literary horizons."

"You don't like mysteries?"

Mane made a regretful *nnn* sound and did a so-so gesture with his hand.

"You know, I wasn't much of a mystery reader when I moved here," Ellery admitted. "I don't think I'd read one since *The Hardy Boys*. And now..."

Mane offered another glimpse of his charming smile. "And now you're a reluctant real-life amateur sleuth."

"And now I'm—" Mane's pager went off, and Ellery finished, "Keeping you from your rounds."

Mane's expression was rueful. "I think it has a sensor that warns it I'm enjoying myself too much."

Ellery wasn't quite sure how to respond to that, and while he was considering and discarding replies, Mane said, "I'll drop by the Crow's Nest one of these days, and you can pick me out a book."

"Medical thriller?"

"Anything but!" Mane grinned and headed off in the opposite direction.

* * * * *

Since he was already out and about, Ellery decided to stop by the Black House on his way back to the Crow's Nest. He could take a quick look around and make sure the house was still safe and secure, clean up the broken glass in the kitchen, and grab the bag of books to deliver to Miss Blackwell on his way home that evening.

The wind had picked up, ruffling the hillside grass and wildflowers, churning the ocean to whitecaps, sending clouds scudding across the endless stretch of blue skies. The VW zipped along the winding dirt road, managing not to hit any hikers or bikers or golf carts that seemed determined to throw themselves in Ellery's path.

He passed Beacon Tower and parked at last in front of the ornate iron gates of the Blackwell Estate.

When he got out of the car, he noticed the chain on the gates had been cut.

Ellery's initial alarm faded as he realized that the paramedics would have had to cut through the chain to gain access to the property. He hadn't given it a thought until now. He pushed the gates wide, folded back into the VW, and continued up the drive to the house.

Everything looked perfectly normal. Okay, maybe not that. No gardener had laid shears or rake to that garden in decades. But everything looked undisturbed since his last visit.

He got out of the car, walked up the steps to the front porch, and let himself in.

For a moment, he stood in the front hall, listening.

He could hear a clock ticking—several clocks ticking—and from outside, a bird singing sweetly. The birdsong reminded him of Pepper Owen and the disastrous end of the previous night's stakeout.

He sighed, imagining Jack's reaction when he shared the story of his adventures, and crossed the hall, heading for the kitchen. He thought he would begin by cleaning up the glass he'd broken on his last visit.

He'd just reached the doorway when someone sneezed.

Ellery froze mid-step.

A man stood in front of the open refrigerator, his back to Ellery. He was tall, about Ellery's height, broad-shouldered and dressed all in black. Black jeans, black turtleneck, black gloves, black ski mask pushed high on his head as he wiped his nose.

The black gloves were what freaked Ellery out.

You didn't have to be a cop or criminologist to know that gloves equaled sinister intent. At least where no snow was involved.

In the split-second before the squeak of the floorboard alerted the intruder to Ellery's presence, Ellery had time to realize he had walked into a potentially dangerous situation. This was no hungry beachcomber forced to resort to B&E to feed himself.

He took a step back at the same time the intruder whirled in startled alarm. He hurled the item he held, with full force, at Ellery's head.

Ellery ducked as a jar of jam smashed against the doorframe, glass and sticky red stuff going everywhere.

He ran for the front door, but the intruder was on top of him before he'd taken three steps. They crashed in front of the grand staircase, and the fight began in earnest. The intruder grabbed a fistful of Ellery's hair and tried to slam his head on the hardwood floor, but Ellery managed to roll onto his side, taking the intruder with him. He directed a hard thrust with the heel of his hand under his attacker's chin, but the chin jab was softened by the lousy angle and the thick, soft ski mask the intruder had pulled down again. He did fall back, but he was not stunned.

Fighting in real life was not like fighting in the movies. In the movies, everything was choreographed and timed perfectly, and as strenuous as it was fighting off pretend ghosts and demons and ax-wielding maniacs, three minutes of a real-life brawl was a million times more exhausting. His heart was hammering like a locomotive, his muscles were shaking with adrenaline and strain, his breathing was all out of control. The blows landing on his chest and back were not pretend. They hurt.

Ellery delivered a couple of good kicks and scrambled to his knees. The intruder grabbed his ankle, Ellery kicked free, and finally managed to regain his feet—just as the intruder did.

As the intruder was blocking Ellery's access to the front door, Ellery turned and sprinted for the kitchen.

As desperate as he was, the intruder was even more so. He dived after Ellery, and they both crashed into the long kitchen table.

Which was painful.

Considerably.

Ellery swore, kicked and punched. He had a dizzying view of a swinging ceiling lamp, a pink cottage-cheese carton, a closet door standing open, and a pair of bloodshot blue eyes boring into his own.

He managed to punch and wriggle free again, delivered a satisfyingly hefty blow to the intruder's face, and sprang for...

There was no door leading outside.

He barely had time to process this before the intruder grabbed him and hurled him through the closet door.

The door did not lead to a closet, however.

Ellery crashed down a flight of rickety wooden steps and landed hard on what felt like bedrock. For a stunned second he lay there, blinking, trying to comprehend what the heck happened. He felt like he'd plummeted through the looking glass onto another planet.

Actually, it was worse. It was the cellar.

He raised his head, shook it, took in the terrifying image of a figure in black silhouetted at the top of the stairs. The next instant, the door slammed shut and the world went dark.

Ellery gasped, tried to get up, had to sit back down for a second. He felt a little dizzy and a little sick. Hopefully, he hadn't just re-concussed himself. He took a couple of deep, slow breaths, and tried again, much more slowly, to rise.

"Ow. Ow. *Ouch.*"

This time he managed to get to his feet. He shuffled cautiously across the pitch-black space, hands outstretched. The toe of his sneakers hit the base of the steps. He felt for and found the rough wood of the banister, and climbed his way up to the top. A razor-sharp band of daylight outlined the frame of the door but cast no real illumination.

He could not hear anything from the other side of the door.

Groping for the door handle, he turned it back and forth, and was not surprised to find it locked. He pounded on the surface.

"Hey!" he shouted. "Open this door!"

That was just venting his frustration. He knew he wasn't going to get an answer, let alone cooperation.

He stepped back to try to put his shoulder to the door, and nearly pitched down the stairs a second time. He'd imagined he was on some kind of landing, but no. He was simply on the top step, and a misguided move was going to send him careening down to the cellar floor.

Ellery swore under his breath, slammed the palm of his hand a final time on the door. He rested his head against the weathered surface, listening again.

It was hard to hear over the thumping of his heart and the blood rushing in his ears. He probably wouldn't have been able to hear a thing through those thick planks anyway. Or maybe there was nothing to hear. Maybe—hopefully—the intruder had fled.

He reached for his phone, praying there would be a signal.

His phone wasn't there.

Even as he patted his jeans, he knew what happened. At some point during the scuffle, he'd dropped his cell.

He swore again. Muttered, "I don't *believe* it." He did believe it, though, because it was the obvious explanation.

Now what? Ellery stood for a moment in the chilly black silence, trying to think. He was still shaking with shock and the adrenaline overload of struggling with his attacker, belatedly starting to feel the scrapes and scratches and bruises he'd sustained.

Think.

There had to be a light switch somewhere. Most likely located near the door.

He began to feel his way across the stone wall, remembering not to step backward, working methodically in small squares: across, down, back. Three squares across the wall, he found the switch and flicked it on.

To his enormous relief, lackluster light radiated from a bare bulb in the cellar below, illuminating mold-stained brick walls, crumbling vaulted ceilings, and wine racks empty of all but a handful of bottles. The floor looked slimy, and there seemed to be an alarming number of dangling electrical cords.

No windows. No other door.

Fan-flipping-tastic.

Slowly, he started down the rickety steps to the basement proper, scanning the dank floor, hoping against hope that he'd dropped his phone in the cellar.

But no.

His phone was not in there.

Oh hell.

Before he was halfway down the steps, he heard it ringing—on the other side of the cellar door.

CHAPTER NINE

Don't go down to the basement.

Words to live by.

But here he was. It could have been worse. He could have broken his neck when he fell down the stairs. The intruder could have had a gun. The light bulb might not have worked. Yeah, being stuck in damp, funky-smelling pitch darkness would not have done his nerves any good.

"Hey! Anybody! Can anybody hear me?"

Of course no one could hear him. The nearest house was Bloodworth Manor House, and that had to be half a mile away. But maybe a hiker? Maybe someone walking their dog? Maybe a renegade bird-watcher?

"Help! Help! Anybody? Is anyone out there?"

His VW was parked outside the house. Someone was bound to see it at some point and come looking for him.

Not that he wanted to wait around for rescue, which might take days to come.

No. It would be preferable all around to get himself out of there as soon as possible.

Ellery made a quick exploration of his prison. The cellar was larger than it looked from above—four rooms larger—and the light from the lonely buzzing bulb did not spread very far, though far enough to verify that his initial impression was right: no windows, no doors beyond the one at the top of the stairs.

So unless he could break down that door or there was a secret passage in there somewhere...

Well, what about a secret passage? Most, if not all, of the Pirate's Eight homes had hidden rooms and secret tunnels.

Granted, the original Black House had burned in the 1880s, so even if there had been a secret passage, it might no longer exist.

From upstairs he could hear his phone ringing again. He listened.

He didn't recognize the ring, so it wasn't Nora or Dylan or Jack or anyone else he was in frequent communication with.

Miss Blackwell maybe?

Someone trying to sell him a timeshare?

A producer offering him the role of a lifetime?

No need to panic. Sooner or later someone close to him was going to wonder where he was and start phoning. He just had to be patient.

He did not feel patient. Standing there—since he wasn't about to sit on that damp, filthy floor—and watching the shadows for any change or movement was not conducive to calm. Just because he knew movies were make-believe didn't mean he wasn't as susceptible to lighting and atmosphere as the next person locked in a spooky cellar.

Not that he expected the ghost of Rufus Blackwell to materialize.

But Miss Blackwell had been genuinely terrified when she'd talked about the ghost.

That crazy laugh, the way her eyes had darted to his and then away, the tremor in her hands... She had not been faking.

Ellery recognized acting when he saw it, and Miss Blackwell had not been acting.

And yet...something had been off there.

She'd been rattled by Sue. That was understandable. Sue used to rattle Ellery too. Sue was like a pit bull once she got an idea in her head, and if she turned out to be wrong, it only made her madder and more determined to prove herself right about her hapless subject the next time.

Had Sue heard that the ghost of Rufus Blackwell had appeared once again? Thus foretelling Miss Blackwell's death?

As much as Ellery would like to think Sue wouldn't stoop to terrorizing old ladies, he knew she wouldn't view her behavior in that light. Sue wouldn't think that speculating on whether Miss Blackwell's ghostly ancestor had predicted her death was in bad taste or cruel or plain old idiotic. She'd argue that the reported appearance of a ghost was news.

Had Miss Blackwell really seen the ghost of Rufus Blackwell?

One thing Miss Blackwell had never seemed was timid or easily spooked.

Ellery glanced up as the ceiling bulb flickered.

Please have paid your electric bill, Miss Blackwell.

He tried yelling again. "Help! Help! Can anyone hear me?" Not that he had much hope anyone was going to hear him, but it did release some of his nervous tension.

At least the last time—and how embarrassing was it that within the space of a month, he'd been locked twice—*twice*—inside an old building? It was *beyond* embarrassing. Anyway, at least the last time, he'd had his phone. He'd been able to summon help.

Ellery made another restless tour of the cellar.

The adjoining rooms were full of broken furniture and discarded building materials blanketed beneath layers of dust and spiderwebs and rodent droppings. If there were any secret passages down here, he'd have to be a lot more desperate before he tried shifting all that junk to find them.

The main part of the cellar was also full of rubbish: a broken TV, a broken bicycle, dusty cardboard boxes of musty, faded clothes. But there were also wine racks (mostly empty) and shelves stacked with rusty and spotted canned goods. Closer inspection revealed that the canned goods were decades old and the remaining wine bottles were empty. It seemed likely Miss Blackwell had not been down to the cellar in years.

And really, why *would* she risk those stairs for some botulin-laced canned pears?

As for a possible secret passage leading to freedom... Not so much. Just like at the Salty Dog, there was a bricked-over section of wall, but the section was much larger than required for a doorway. Given the water stains and mold, it looked to Ellery like the supporting wall had started to give way at some point and had been hastily repaired.

Hopefully *well* repaired.

Without his cell, it was hard to judge the passing of time.

It felt like he'd been locked in the cellar forever when Ellery heard Nora's muffled ringtone from upstairs.

He listened tensely as she tried calling three times in a row. Then silence.

Okay. That was good. That was hopeful. Nora would not shrug off being unable to reach him. Nora would persist.

About—maybe?—thirty minutes after Nora tried to phone him, he heard Jack's ringtone.

He counted the rings aloud.

One.

Two.

Three.

Four.

Five.

Six.

Silence.

Ellery let out a long breath.

By now, he was past the point of worrying what Jack would think of his predicament. He just wanted *out*. The dust was making him sneeze, his stomach had been growling for hours, he would have liked to use the restroom, and he'd resorted to leaning against the staircase because, as tired as he was of standing, the thought of sitting down and risking spiders crawling into his underwear was just too horrific. Worst of all, the light bulb overhead had started buzzing in a way that did not bode well for the evening's entertainment.

Jack did not try phoning again.

Ellery was not sure if that was good news or bad news.

He decided once again to see if he could find something to use as a tool to get through the door. It seemed impossible that somewhere in all this trash, there wouldn't be a shovel or a crowbar or even a screwdriver.

Sometime later, he was forced to admit that if there was something useful down here, he sure couldn't find it. He couldn't locate so much as a wire hanger.

If someone didn't show up pretty soon... How long *had* he been down here?

His phone began to ring again. Jack's ringtone. His heart leaped in hope at the faint squeaking sound overhead. Were those footsteps?

He charged up the stairs and began hammering on the door.

"Hey! Hello? Over here! I'm in here!"

Just when he thought that his hand would go numb from hitting the door so hard, he heard Jack's voice on the other side of the door.

"Ellery? Hold on."

Ellery stepped back from the door, expecting Jack to crash it down. Instead, he heard a *click*, and the door opened to reveal Jack standing there, panting heavily as if he *had* kicked the door in. He looked Ellery up and down as though verifying he was still in one piece, and then opened his mouth.

"Before you say anything—" Ellery said quickly.

"Are you okay?"

"Yes. I'm fine."

Jack didn't seem to hear him. His eyes looked dark in his pale face. "Is that blood in your hair?"

Ellery reached up, touched something sticky, examined his scarlet fingers, and noticed tiny seeds. "Jam."

"*Jam?*"

"There could be cottage cheese too, for all I know."

Jack stared at Ellery's sticky, red fingers, blinked, and shouted, *"What in the hell is going on?"*

"What do you think is going on? Why are you yelling at me?"

That seemed to leave Jack speechless. He spluttered, "What do I— Why am I—"

As Jack seemed rooted in place, Ellery edged around him, looking around the kitchen for his phone. "There was someone here when I arrived. We struggled, and he shoved me in the cellar and locked the door."

He was startled to see the kitchen looked like it had been wrecked. The table was shoved halfway down the room, chairs were scattered everywhere, and more broken glass had been added to that of his original visit.

Jack stepped in front of him. "What do you mean *someone was here*? What were *you* doing here in the first place?"

"I don't understand why you're mad at me. It's not like I planned this."

"I'm relieved to hear it!"

"I was here to pick up some books. That's the only reason—"

"Oh, give me a break." Jack's tone was disgusted. "Once again you're playing amateur sleuth, and once again you're putting your safety at risk."

"No, Jack. That's not fair. I didn't have an ulterior motive."

"You're barely recovered from the last time you stuck your nose where it didn't belong."

That was perfectly true. And perfectly irritating.

"Jack, I'm telling you the truth. I came here to pick up the books I delivered to Miss Blackwell yesterday to bring them to her in the hospital. She *asked* me to come here. I was doing her a favor, and that's *all* I was doing."

"If that's true—"

"*If* that's true?" Ellery did not like confrontation. He was slow to anger and quick to get over being mad. But after what he'd been through, the skepticism in Jack's voice and expression made his blood boil. "Hey, if you think I'm a liar, so be it." He finally spotted his phone lying against the baseboard next to the sink and brushed past Jack.

Jack caught his arm, and Ellery turned to face him, scowling.

"I don't think you're a liar." Jack made an effort to speak more calmly. "And I don't want to fight with you."

"I don't want to fight with you either."

Jack's frown faded. His shoulders relaxed a little, and he let go of Ellery's arm. "So let's *not* fight. Tell me what happened. Start from your decision to come here."

Ellery stared straight into Jack's blue-green eyes. "It's exactly how I told you. Miss Blackwell *asked* me to come by the house, pick up the books

I delivered yesterday, and bring them to her in the hospital."

Jack said nothing.

"Do I think she's nervous about someone breaking in again and was privately hoping I'd be able to reassure her that no one had been here? Yes. I do. I think she's frightened. And I don't blame her, given what just happened to me."

Jack let out a long, controlled breath. "Okay. Fair enough. I'm sorry I jumped to the wrong conclusion." He couldn't help adding, "This time."

Ellery glowered. "I'm not looking for trouble. I'm really not."

"And yet trouble keeps finding you."

"You think I'm happy about that?"

Jack regarded him, said with wry honesty, "I'm not sure."

"Swell!"

Jack ignored that. "Did you get a look at your attacker?"

"Yes."

Jack's face lightened. "Great. Did you recognize him? Do you have a name?"

"No. No, I didn't recognize him. That doesn't mean he isn't local. There are plenty of people on this island I've never seen, let alone met." He bent to retrieve his phone, pocketed it.

Jack took out his trusty notebook. "Okay. Let's have it."

"My height. Six feet. But heavier. He's in good shape. Maybe mid-forties. Maybe older. He was wearing a ski mask pushed back on his head. He dragged it down over his face as soon as he saw me, but I did see his face. It was kind of long and narrow. Good cheekbones."

Jack sighed.

Ellery said, "I'm trying to tell you everything I remember while it's still clear in my mind."

"Go on."

"I think his hair was light brown or maybe sandy blond. Maybe bleached? He had...stubble."

"A beard?"

"Maybe that's the goal. He definitely hasn't shaved for a few days. His eyes were blue. Blue and bloodshot."

"Did he speak?"

"Grunts. Swearing."

"Could you detect an accent? Would you recognize his voice if you heard it again?"

"I don't think so. I doubt it. We were wrestling, so it wasn't his normal voice." Ellery added ruefully, "It wasn't my normal voice either." In fact, he was still hoarse from his bouts of shouting for help.

Jack's gaze flicked up to Ellery's and then back to his notebook. "Was there something distinctive about the way he moved?"

"You mean beside rushing to attack me? Not that I could tell. He was fast and fit."

Jack made a note. "Anything else you can re-member? Anything at all?"

"I don't think so."

"What did he smell like?"

"What did he *smell* like?" Ellery cast his mind back to those few fraught seconds of wrestling in the kitchen. "Anxious? He was perspiring heavily, which is understandable. It's almost eighty today, and he was wearing black from head to toe. I don't think he's bathed recently."

"Hmm." Jack scratched another couple of notes.

Ellery hunted for and found the bag of books he'd dropped outside the kitchen. "By the way, how did you know to come looking for me?"

"Nora put out an APB."

"What?"

"Nora phoned when you didn't come back from the hospital. She was worried."

"And you guessed I'd be here?"

"Yes. I did. I figured you'd want to return to the scene of the crime."

That was irritating because it had not been Ellery's choice to return to the Black House. But he let it go. He appreciated the fact that Jack had dropped everything to come and look for him.

Jack flipped his notebook shut. "All right. I'm going to have a look around and figure out how our perp got in. Then I've got to file a report and speak to Miss Blackwell, so it's going to be more like seven thirty or eight."

Ellery asked blankly, "What's going to be more like seven thirty?"

"Dinner." Jack's expression changed. "Unless—"

"Are we still having dinner?" Ellery was startled.

Jack said stiffly, "Not if you don't want to."

"No, I want to. I just assumed you weren't in the mood to socialize."

Jack hesitated. "I still want to have dinner." He didn't sound very sure about it, though.

"Yes," Ellery said quickly. "Heck yeah, we're still on. Seven thirty is fine. Whenever is fine."

He was very glad Jack had not decided to cancel dinner. He suspected Jack was still not happy with him, but at least he wasn't backing off. That was a relief.

They walked in silence to the front door. When they reached the door, Ellery stopped.

"What?" Jack asked.

"I just remembered something."

"What did you remember?"

"When I walked into the kitchen, the door to the refrigerator was open, and the intruder was standing there eating what looked like jam and cottage cheese."

"That's..."

"Truly heinous, I know."

Jack's lips twitched. "I was going to say interesting."

"That too. He threw the jam jar at me."

"There's an empty cottage-cheese container sitting on the kitchen counter."

"That definitely wasn't there yesterday. Maybe this guy has a serious cottage cheese and jelly addiction," Ellery said. "Or *maybe* he's hungry."

Jack didn't laugh. "Maybe he is," he agreed.

CHAPTER TEN

"**T**hank heavens you're all right!" Nora exclaimed when Ellery walked into the Crow's Nest a little after six.

"A funny thing happened on the way to get Miss Blackwell her books."

Watson practically fell over his feet in his rush to get to Ellery. His whimpers sounded strangled as he braced his front paws on Ellery's legs, begging to be picked up.

"Hey, what's all this about?" Ellery picked Watson up and cuddled him. "Did you think I'd abandoned you?"

Watson frantically licked Ellery's chin and face, so the answer seemed to be *yes*.

"Thanks for sending Jack," Ellery told Nora. "If he hadn't shown up, I'd still be sitting in Miss Blackwell's haunted basement, counting the spiders."

"*Haunted?*"

"Well, atmospheric."

"What on earth happened?"

Ellery told her the entire story from start to finish.

At the end of his recital, Nora, predictably, seemed more intrigued than concerned.

"Miss Blackwell's intruder doesn't seem to have been in any hurry."

"No. He didn't. He was definitely surprised to see me. Which means he knew Miss Blackwell is in the hospital. He wasn't expecting any interruptions."

"I don't suppose you could tell what was missing from the house?"

Ellery thought back, tried to visualize walking through the front hall of the Black House. "I wasn't there, or at least wasn't upstairs, long enough to be sure. But I don't know that anything *was* missing."

"What do you mean?"

"Well, for example, when the Barbys were being burgled, it was obvious. There were signs of staging inside the house. The burglars had gathered everything they were taking in the front room. They had a vehicle to move the heavier items, like televisions and safes and electronics. They had boxes to put wine in. Paintings were stacked together. Here, it didn't seem like anything was out of place, and there wasn't so much as a backpack in sight."

"Maybe he'd just arrived."

"That's possible. He knew he had plenty of time, and so he decided to have a snack before he got to work. I didn't see any car or bike or any kind of transportation, but maybe he didn't have far to travel."

"And it seems he works alone."

"Yes. It does seem that way."

"That raises a number of possibilities," Nora said thoughtfully. "By the way, I rescheduled the interviews you missed."

Ellery groaned. "Blowing off an interview. That's bound to impress any prospective employee."

Nora brushed that off. "It's an employer's market on this island." She gathered her belongings. "Have a good evening, dearie."

"Thanks for staying late, Nora."

Her smile was unexpectedly affectionate. "So long as you're all right. That's the main thing."

* * * * *

Since he still had to stop by the grocery store to pick up dinner, Ellery decided Miss Blackwell would have to wait one more evening for her books.

He made a quick trip to the market to pick up beer, chicken, tomatoes, fresh parsley and other herbs, as well as Jack's favorite ice cream for dessert. By now he knew Jack well enough to know what Jack liked to eat. He was not as health conscious as Ellery, but he did appreciate simple, good food and home-cooked meals, which was kind of Ellery's specialty.

When they arrived at Captain's Seat, Ellery let Watson out, allowed him to run loose for a few minutes, and then he carried the groceries inside. He fed

Watson, who attacked every meal as though it might be his last.

Enough time had passed that Ellery was feeling the aches and pains of his fight with Miss Blackwell's intruder. He poured himself a glass of wine, ran a very hot bath, dumped in a couple of cups of Epsom salts, and settled in the tub for a quick game of Scrabble GO and a nice, relaxing soak.

Either he was having trouble focusing, or the Scrabble Oracle was having an off week, because the digital tile arrangements remained exasperatingly random.

Coldhearted, cold, case, vengeful, testament, date, night—Jack did not enjoy games, which was a pity because Strip Scrabble was a thing—KISS, KILL...

Maybe Scrabble Go was channeling Jack's feelings?

When Ellery hauled himself out of the tub and dressed, he was feeling a whole lot better in body, mind, and spirit.

Downstairs in the kitchen, he seasoned the chicken pieces with salt and pepper on all sides, used his food processor to pulverize the herbs and capers for the Italian-style salsa verde, and set about chopping the tomatoes for the tomato salad.

Having had time to reflect, he'd started questioning the likelihood of *two* hungry prowlers operating in Pirate's Cove. It seemed like a stretch. But if

Miss Blackwell's intruder and Libby's intruder were one and the same...that was even more puzzling.

What, beyond refrigerators, could the Salty Dog pub and Miss Blackwell possibly have in common?

Maybe the kitchens of other homes and businesses were also being raided?

Granted, Libby's prowler took money and booze as well as food. It was unclear whether Miss Blackwell was missing anything beyond cottage cheese and jam.

Here was a question. Who dressed up like a cat burglar to steal food?

The more Ellery thought about it, the more he wondered whether Miss Blackwell *had* seen the intruder, which was why she'd wanted him to go and make sure her home was still safe to return to. But then, why make up that story about the ghost of Rufus Blackwell appearing to her?

Or *had* she made that up? Because she'd seemed genuinely frightened.

Then again, the idea of an intruder would be legitimately alarming too.

Could she have confused the intruder with an apparition?

That seemed unlikely. Despite her penchant for day drinking, Miss Blackwell had always seemed perfectly sharp.

Could both things be true? Had the ghost of Rufus Blackwell appeared at the same time someone broke into the Black House?

Yeah. No.

He'd felt yesterday that Miss Blackwell might be, well, prevaricating a little. And there could be any number of harmless reasons for that. Despite her flirtatiousness, she might not trust him completely. The house was full of collectibles, if not actual valuables. Maybe she was paranoid about people being after her stuff. Or she might have embarrassing secrets she was concerned about having revealed, like the fact that the family fortune wasn't what it once was.

Difficult to know.

It was more than reasonable that someone who'd lived as a recluse for decades might have trust issues. Might find the world outside her imposing gates quite alarming, even threatening.

Or maybe Sue was onto something. Maybe Miss Blackwell was cheating on her social security or committing Medicare fraud?

Or maybe Sue was as delusional about Miss Blackwell as she'd been about him.

In any case, Ellery's sympathy was now tempered by his uneasy suspicion that Miss Blackwell had guessed he might encounter her prowler. Maybe he was being unfair. Even if it was true, he couldn't blame her for hoping someone younger, stronger, and male might run interference for her.

Still.

Ellery was on the back terrace, grilling the chicken, when Jack arrived at a quarter to eight.

Watson, of course, gave Ellery plenty of warning before Jack came around the side of the house. The pup threw himself down the steps and greeted Jack in his customary running circles around him and then jumping up and down.

But then, that was how most of Pirate's Cove greeted Jack.

"Hey there!" Ellery waved his barbecue tongs in greeting. The Weber grill was a recent purchase from the Target in Newport, and most nights Jack came for dinner, Ellery grilled and they ate outside.

Jack had taken time to shower, shave, and change into jeans and a white T-shirt with a spinning black vinyl record logo. Jack's taste in T-shirts frequently reminded Ellery that he still had a lot to learn about Jack. Which, for the, er, record, he looked forward to.

Jack had picked up a bottle of wine. Ellery took the grooming and wine as indications that Jack was sorry about their earlier run-in. Ellery was also sorry, which was why he'd sprung for mocha-pecan ice-cream bonbons. Jack had once admitted they were a guilty pleasure.

"Hi." Jack joined Ellery on the terrace and kissed his cheek. He held up the bottle of Rodney Strong cab. "I guessed red." He glanced at the grilling chicken. "I guessed wrong."

"Wine is never wrong." Was Jack *maybe* a little self-conscious? Ellery said, "How was Miss Blackwell?"

"Wishing I were you." Jack's gaze was teasing. "She told me several times how sorry she was you got thrown in her death trap of a cellar."

"Was she able to give you any idea who her intruder might be?"

Jack's brows rose. "You think she knows who broke into her house?"

Ellery sighed. "I don't know. I've been thinking about the whole situation, and something about it gives me a funny feeling."

"Yeah. Well, she's an eccentric, no question. Did you want a glass of wine?"

"There's an open bottle of white in the fridge. And a six-pack of Heady Topper."

Jack's sudden smile was very white in his tanned face, and Ellery knew it was going to be a good evening.

In fact, it *was* a good evening.

The fresh tomato salad was a perfect pairing for the chicken topped with its herby caper salsa. Ellery and Jack ate and talked and smiled as the sunset grayed to twilight and twilight deepened into night. The fireflies flitted over the meadow, and the occasional shooting star flicked across the sky and disappeared.

"I spoke to my mom last night," Ellery said toward the end of the meal. "She and my dad are planning on visiting next month."

"When?" Jack asked. "I'd like to meet them."

That was so easy, it almost took Ellery aback. "She said she'll let me know, but they're planning on staying about a week."

"There's plenty to do this time of year. It's a good time to visit, so long as they don't mind a crowd."

"One thing my mother doesn't mind is a crowd."

Jack considered Ellery. "She's an actress, right?"

"Yes. Talia Alexander. And George is a director."

Clearly neither name meant anything to Jack. He shook his head. But then neither of Ellery's parents were big box office. That honor had fallen, briefly, to Ellery. The *Happy Halloween! You're Dead!* films had not been critically acclaimed, but they *had* made a lot of money.

Ellery pushed his empty plate aside. "I meant to tell you earlier, but Libby has"—he made air quotes—"hired me to find out if someone is sneaking into the Salty Dog at night."

"*What?* Why would you wait to tell me that?"

"I kept meaning to, but we haven't had a lot of time to talk."

Jack tilted his head in, *Seriously?*

Ellery told Jack the whole story, ending with, "Honestly, I didn't bother you with it because I didn't think there was anything to it. I sort of suspected Libby of asking for attention."

"But you don't any longer?"

"I don't know. That's the truth. She's been through a lot over the past couple of months. The breakup with Felix, Ned's arrest, the stress of leaving home for the first time—the stress of deciding she *wouldn't* leave home for the first time—and now her dad's illness, which leaves the entire responsibility of running the pub on her. I think it's a lot for her to process."

"Then you *do* think she's making up this midnight prowler?"

Ellery grimaced. "After today, I'm not so sure."

Jack looked surprised. "Wait a minute. You think Libby's prowler and Miss Blackwell's are one and the same?"

"It's pretty far-fetched, I know."

Jack said slowly, "Maybe not."

"Really?"

"There's something very weird about this guy. I checked the Blackwell House after you left, and I can't figure out how he got in. The house was locked up tight, and the numbered pieces of paper I left between the side door and the frame were still there—and still in the order I left them."

Ellery chuckled. "You hid slips of paper in the doorframe? That's pure Hardy Boys."

"Believe me, I know. But I don't believe in ghosts. Miss Blackwell's story was flimsier than wet toilet paper, and when you phoned me, you were pretty sure someone had been in the house."

"And someone clearly had, but how is he getting in?"

"Presumably the same way he's getting into the Salty Dog. The tunnels."

Ellery said, "I thought of that, but Tom blocked off the tunnel leading to the Salty Dog when Libby was small. He was afraid she'd get lost down there. I saw where the entrance had been closed off."

"Hmm." Jack looked unconvinced.

"On the other hand, the Black House is one of the Pirate's Eight, so it's more than possible it has a secret passage or two leading outside the estate gates."

Jack considered, said, "One thing I can tell you for sure, Tom is not going to be happy when he hears about Libby hiring you to act as her night watchman."

"True. Which is why I think it's better he hears about it later than sooner, because the kid's right. The minute she tells him, he'll be back at work."

Jack's expression was disapproving. "Tom's a big boy. He should be allowed to make that decision for himself."

"I keep hoping that if I humor her, Libby will tell me what's really going on."

Jack said, "It's possible Libby doesn't know."

CHAPTER ELEVEN

Ellery returned from plating their dessert and set the dish of bonbons in front of Jack, whose brows shot up, before he smiled a funny kind of smile.

"I can't remember the last time someone bought me an ice cream."

Ellery smiled back, but he was touched by Jack's surprised pleasure. Jack was so good at taking care of everyone else, it was easy to forget he deserved to be looked after too.

They ate their ice cream in a sudden silence, spoons scraping glass and cricket song their only soundtrack.

Jack finished his bonbons, put his spoon down. "I want you to understand something." His tone was abrupt.

Ellery sighed. He'd known this was coming.

"No, see, that's what I'm trying to address," Jack said. "I'm not trying to...control you. This isn't territorial, or me not wanting you involved in my work life. I *like* that you're curious and interested and willing to help your friends and neighbors. I think you're a-a good citizen."

"Gosh. That's...the nicest thing anyone's ever said to me."

But Jack didn't laugh, didn't smile. He said quite earnestly, "Don't turn this into a joke, Ellery. Because I'm serious. This is important."

"Okay. Sorry."

"Thanks to the internet, amateur sleuthing is a rising trend in the general population and something that law enforcement has to contend with."

"You're kidding."

Jack looked faintly exasperated. "Now how can *you*, of all people, say that?"

"I'm not an amateur sleuth. I just keep getting dragged into things."

"Which lead you to start sleuthing. This is the fourth time in almost as many months."

Ellery was silent. Jack had a point.

Jack studied his face. "This isn't an intervention, as much as I wish that were possible. You are who you are, and I *like* who you are. Very much."

Now *that* was a compliment, and Ellery's face warmed. "I like you too."

"I'm concerned for your safety. That's what this is about. That's what today was about. That's *all* this is about. You're not operating anonymously behind the wall of the world wide web. You're speaking directly with people. You're blithely strolling into ice houses and graveyards and crypts without telling anyone where you're going. People know who you are. They know where you work. They know where you live."

Ellery opened his mouth, but Jack kept talking. "And I know that it's not always planned, and that things happen, *but* the fact that you're willing to involve yourself in potentially dangerous situations means you *have* to be extra vigilant, extra conscientious about being smart and staying safe."

Ellery considered, was forced to admit that Jack was right, and nodded.

"You know, a cop radios in when they're headed to a possible situation. A cop waits for backup."

"Okay. I get it. I really do."

"I don't *ever* want to go through what I did the night I found you in the Bloodworths' crypt."

"I know. I'm sorry. That would have been aw—"

"I thought you were dead," Jack said harshly. "Those first few seconds..." He shook his head.

They had talked about that night before, but not like this. Knowing what he now did about Jack's tragic history, Ellery could see how that evening must have been traumatic. Especially since Jack believed it was his duty to ensure the safety of every single person on the island.

"Jack." Ellery put his hand over Jack's. "I'm sorry. I'm truly sorry. I give you my word, I'll be more careful in the future. I'll be better about communicating where I am and what I'm up to."

Jack turned his palm up, capturing Ellery's hand in his own. "That's all I'm asking. Proceed with caution."

"I will."

"*And* communicate anything you learn to me."

"Wellll…"

Jack's brows drew together, and Ellery squeezed his hand. "I'm joking. I promise I'll communicate anything I learn, whether I think you'd find it relevant or not."

"Thank you."

"Yeah, well, be careful what you wish for."

Jack's smile tugged into that rare sweet grin. "I don't have any complaints so far."

* * * * * *

"Will it bother you if I read for a while? I can go downstairs."

Jack's eyes blinked open. He turned his head on the pillow.

"I can sleep through anything. What would bother me is if you went downstairs and left me marooned in this bed." His smile was quizzical.

Ellery considered the enormous bed. "I used to lose Watson in here."

Watson, tucked against his side, twitched his ears, though his eyes remained closed.

"I believe it. I feel like we could set sail for the New World in this."

True enough. And the fact that the ginormous bed, with its mortal-combat-ready bedposts and ornate facade-sized headboard, took up so little real estate was an indication of how large the master bedroom was. Ellery had performed in theaters that were smaller.

He reached for his book on the nightstand, dislodging Watson, who rose, shook himself, and curled up against Jack with a reproachful sigh.

Ellery flipped through the book's table of contents, pausing at the gorgeous frontispiece illustration of Tom Blood.

"What are you reading? *Treasure Island*?"

"In a way. This is the 1923 edition of *Pirates of New England*. I found it in Great-great-great-aunt Eudora's library."

Ellery had yet to fully explore the musty, dusty library with its scattered papers, rotting rolls of maps, and thousands of crumbling leather-bound volumes crammed in haphazard order on sagging shelves. As far as renovating the house went, the library was low priority. But he had come across a couple of valuable reference books on his occasional forays into that wood-pulp wilderness, including a vintage guidebook of Buck Island and *Pirates of New England*.

"Nice illustration."

"That's Tom Blood himself. Yeah, the illustrations are beautiful. The book has turned out to be a kind of a bible for the Pirate's Eight."

"You're researching Rufus Blackwell?"

"Yep."

Jack cocked an eyebrow. "Because?"

Ellery shrugged. "Well, Rufus is a starting point for Miss Blackwell's ghost."

"I don't buy the ghost story." Jack had said earlier he didn't believe in ghosts.

"You don't believe in ghosts at all?"

Jack frowned, considered. "Let's put it this way. I don't believe in Miss Blackwell's ghost. In fact, I don't believe anything Miss Blackwell told me."

Jack had plenty of experience in both interviews and interrogations. Ellery figured his assessment was probably correct, not least because it corroborated his own suspicions. "She seemed genuinely frightened."

"That, I'll give you. She's frightened of something, all right. And it seems like she had good reason to be. But a ghost didn't lock you in that cellar."

No. Ellery had the bruises to prove it. He nodded, finished skimming the table of contents. There was no chapter on Rufus Blackwell. A minor player, then, in the game of Black Flag. He checked the index, found a couple of references, and flipped to the pages.

Unlike so many of his contemporaries, Blackwell had been born in New England and had family in Newport. He began his career privateering against French and Spanish ships. The details of when or why he'd moved from privateering to piracy were lost to time, but a friendship with the governor of the

Province of New York had served him well—until it hadn't.

Blackwell captained the *Golden Vanity* and frequently conducted his raids in "consort" with Thomas Swann, captain of the *Bachelor's Delight*. Blackwell and Swann seemed to have been efficient and modestly successful pirates. Their exploits were not particularly daring or violent, but they were sufficiently annoying for the Crown to issue warrants for their arrest.

After Swann went down with his ship off Delaware Bay, Blackwell retired to Buck Island, where he lived quietly off his ill-gotten gains for a couple of years until his younger brother, who had once sailed alongside him, was captured off the coast of New England and, to save his skin, turned King's evidence.

That seemed to have been where the trouble started. Or at least where Miss Blackwell's troubles started.

Rufus, naturally, had not taken kindly to being betrayed by his own kith and kin. After he was tried and sentenced to hang, he reportedly cursed his brother Philip and all his progeny through the ages. And, if that had not been clear enough, on the morning of his hanging, Rufus had reiterated the curse and added a few hair-raising embellishments about his relatives dying a terrible death upon thrice seeing his ghastly visage, etc., etc.

Had that really happened? Hard to say.

Philip Blackwell did not seem consumed with guilt or particularly concerned with the curse. No sooner did he receive his pardon, than he set about usurping his unmarried brother's lands and fortune, and prepared to live happily ever after.

It didn't quite work out that way. The girl Philip planned on marrying died of a fever a week before their wedding. Philip's wife died delivering his third child. His firstborn son choked to death at age six. A year later, Philip fell off his horse and broke his neck.

That was a string of bad luck for any one family. Most of it seemed to have landed on the heads of those who had absolutely nothing to do with the betrayal of Rufus Blackwell, but who could say curses followed a logical course of action?

As far as Ellery could tell, the whispers about the curse began around the time of Rufus's death, but the ghost story seemed to have ignited (no pun intended) when the original Blackwell mansion burned to the ground in the nineteenth century. Witnesses claimed to see the figure of Rufus Blackwell standing in the windows of the mansion.

And that was pretty much all *Pirates of New England* had to say on the matter. The author had been interested in the actions of living pirates, not dead ones. If Ellery wanted to learn more about the ghost of Rufus Blackwell, he'd have to find some other source material.

He thought again of Great-great-great-aunt Eudora's library, but if he didn't feel like venturing in there during the daylight, he sure as heck didn't want to try poking around close to midnight.

No, his ghost-hunting would have to wait until the next day.

He turned out the lamp and scooted down between the sheets.

Jack hooked an arm around him, pulled him close, kissed his temple.

They breathed in peaceful unison.

The owl that nested in the garret was *who-who-ing* from the red maple tree outside the window.

Ellery thought Jack was asleep again, but Jack murmured, "It's so quiet out here."

"Sometimes, when the wind's right, you can hear the ocean."

"Nice."

Ellery nodded.

"That was one of the things I had trouble getting used to," Jack said. "How quiet the nights were."

"Same."

He'd been lonely when he'd first moved to Pirate's Cove. Captain's Seat was so remote, so isolated, but even when Ellery was in the village, working at the bookshop, he'd been essentially on his own. At the time, he'd believed the people of Pirate's Cove were keeping their distance. And certainly after Trevor Maple's murder, they *had* kept a distance.

Now, though, he realized that much of the distance had been of his own making. Still angry and still hurt by Todd's betrayal, he'd been wary of making connections with others.

But he had been lonely. Not for Todd. God no. But for companionship. Friendship.

And now he had all that and more.

Who? asked the owl again. *Who?*

Ellery smiled.

It was nice like this. Nice having someone to share his bed. For all the obvious reasons. But for the less obvious reasons too. Like having someone to talk to late at night. Like the comfort of waking from a bad dream and hearing someone breathing peacefully beside you. Like the happy surprise of someone waking you with a kiss.

CHAPTER TWELVE

Libby was waiting when Ellery arrived at the Crow's Nest the next morning.

"He's back! He stole my meat loaf!"

Now there was something you didn't hear every day.

Ellery unlocked the door. The bell rang out in cheerful dissonance as Watson pushed the door wide. Ellery beckoned Libby inside.

"All right, all right. Tell me exactly what happened."

"It's just the same as before. I didn't see anyone or anything on the security footage, but he was *there*. The entire meat loaf is *gone*."

"If you didn't see anyone, how do you know the intruder isn't a *she*?"

Libby looked startled. "You think the thief is Pepper Owen?"

No. He really didn't. Not after his experience at the Black House the day before. He was speaking for the sake of argument. He was stalling because he knew she was not going to like what he had to say.

"Libby, you've got to tell your dad about this."

Her eyes widened in alarm. "*No.* I told you why I can't do that."

Ellery let out a long, exasperated breath. "I understand your concern. Kind of. But your dad is going to be mad as hell when he finds out, which he will."

"No, he won't."

"*Of course* he will, and I'm the one he's going to be mad at, and rightfully so, because I'm the adult here."

She opened her mouth, but Ellery wasn't through. "Plus, your dad might have the answer to all this. He might have an idea who's breaking in."

"They're not *breaking* in."

"You know what I mean. And he might know *how* they're getting in. Because I just don't believe that someone is timing their entry to crawl through the doorway, disarm the system, sneak around the cameras into the kitchen, steal food and whatever, and then crawl out again. It's..."

Insane. He didn't say it, though.

Her eyes shone with tears. "I'm not making it up!"

"I know you're not." Until that moment, he hadn't been one hundred percent sure, but he was now. And if her prowler was real, and Miss Blackwell's prowler was *definitely* real, well, there was no way that *two* intruders were sneaking around Pirate's

Cove stealing food. Money, alcohol, maybe, but the theft of food—Miss Blackwell's intruder had been in the act of *eating* when Ellery discovered him—indicated something different. This wasn't another burglary ring or even the remnants of the old burglary ring.

This was...weird.

This did not fit a recognizable pattern. Even Jack was puzzled by it.

Which reminded Ellery.

"Also, even if I wanted to keep concealing this situation from your dad, Chief Carson knows about it."

"What?" She flushed angrily. "You told Chief Carson? *Him*? Of all people—"

"*Libby.*" She broke off at the unusual sharpness of his tone. "What's happening at the Salty Dog is a crime. I can't lie to Jack."

"I didn't ask you to lie. But you didn't have to go out of your way to tell him."

"It's not that simple. There's a possibility that what's happening at the pub is tied in to the break-in at Miss Blackwell's. If I didn't tell Jack, I would be concealing evidence."

Or something like that. He wasn't exactly sure himself.

Libby looked startled at this information. "I thought there wasn't a break-in at Miss Blackwell's?"

"It turns out, there was. And there may be more in the village, for all we know. So can you see why

I couldn't keep that information to myself when it might be relevant to an ongoing investigation?"

She said finally, grudgingly, "Yes." And then added, "Is he going to tell my dad about the prowler?"

"I don't know. Knowing Jack, probably? I'm not sure. He didn't say. He didn't like the fact that we were keeping Tom in the dark about this."

She scowled. "He should mind his own business."

"This *is* his business. He's the police chief."

She looked unconvinced but didn't argue. An idea seemed to come to her. "You must be close to solving it by now. Can't he hold off for a day or so? Pop's so much better now."

"I'm *nowhere* close to solving this." Ellery studied her, sighed. "I can talk to Jack, ask him to wait twenty-four hours. Not that I see the point, but I don't suppose it will do any harm. Jack—Chief Carson— might not agree, though. It's his call."

"He'll hold off if *you* ask him," Libby said with unexpected shrewdness.

"*Hmph,*" Ellery replied, and opened the door for her.

"What do you know about the ghost of Rufus Blackwell?" Ellery asked Nora over coffee that morning.

Nora's face lit with enthusiasm. "It's one of our best ghost stories!"

"I read a little about it in *Pirates of New England* last night."

"Oh, there won't be much in there. The historical society used to sell a wonderful little book called *Ghosts of Buck Island.* I have a copy at home. I'm sure Eudora had a copy as well."

"I haven't had a chance to look through the library."

"There are wonderful things in that library." Nora's eyes gleamed at the thought of Great-great-great-aunt Eudora's book graveyard. "You're in for a treat."

Also silicosis.

Ellery kept that thought to himself, and said, "So the first appearance of the ghost was when the Blackwell house burned down?"

"No! Oh no." Nora was definite. "There had been many sightings of Rufus before the original house burned. In fact, according to legend, Philip Blackwell threatened to beat to death any servant who spoke of seeing the ghost of his brother."

"He really was kind of an all-round jerk, wasn't he?"

"He really was. Also, not very smart. When you forbid people to speak of something, naturally, it's all they can talk about, and that seems to have been the case with the ghost of Rufus."

"According to Miss Blackwell and *Pirates of New England*, when the ghost of Rufus appears three times to someone, they die."

Nora shook her head. "That part of the legend seems to have developed later on."

"Rufus didn't say that as he was about to be hanged?"

"It's hard to know. But the details of the curse first show up in *Pirates of New England*. There's nothing so specific in the earlier accounts. It might be true, but it's hard to believe a hangman allowing his prisoner to make a long speech and then finish up by delivering a curse, especially given that Rufus was hung with twenty-five other pirates that day. I can't imagine there was a lot of time for chitchat."

Now that was a fresh perspective.

"Miss Blackwell seems to believe in that part of the story. She said her father saw Rufus's ghost three times before he died, and that the same thing happened to her grandfather, but she didn't believe it until she saw the ghost herself."

"It is her ghost, after all," Nora said. "One doesn't like to argue with the haunted."

Ellery kept a straight face. "When do *you* believe the ghost of Rufus first appeared?"

Nora rubbed her hands together with the glee of a pitcher about to deliver a four-seam fastball. "It was a dark and stormy night when Philip arrived on the island to take possession of his murdered brother's estate. They say he tried every door to the mansion, but none would open. At last, he went around to the side entrance for tradesmen, and *that* door allowed him entry to the house."

Dissed from beyond the grave. Ouch.

Ellery grinned. "It was a dark and stormy night? Really?"

"Artistic license. Anyway. When Philip reached the library, he found a fire burning merrily in the grate and a glass of French brandy sitting on a table beside his brother's favorite chair. A portrait of Rufus hung over the fireplace, and Philip could see the shadow of flames dancing in the portrait's eyes. Philip fainted straight away."

"You don't really think of retired pirates as being the fainted-straight-away kind," Ellery objected.

Nora gave him a chiding look. "When Philip regained his senses the next morning—"

"The next *morning*?"

"He found a letter addressed to him by his dead brother. *The ink was still wet.*"

"Still wet? How long was the letter? Had Rufus just finished writing it?"

Nora sighed.

"Sorry. What did the letter say?"

"No one knows."

"There weren't any witnesses to all this?"

"No."

Ellery laughed. "So this is totally made up?"

Nora twinkled. "Yes. Sadly. It's a wonderful story, though. The book is delightful. I'll loan you my copy."

"I'd like to read it. What's the actual legend?"

"According to contemporary accounts, when Philip walked into the master's chamber, Rufus was waiting for him, and Philip fainted straight away. We know this because his valet witnessed it. The faint, not the specter. That was the first official sighting of Rufus's ghost."

"And you use the term *official* loosely?"

"As loose as a hangman's noose."

"Hm."

Nora said, "According to legend, Rufus's ghost was seen frequently by servants and visitors, but Philip never again admitted to seeing his brother's apparition. He forbade anyone to speak of Rufus or the ghost."

"Guilty conscience."

"No doubt."

"The Blackwells do seem to have been pretty unlucky."

"Yes, starting with Rufus," Nora pointed out. "He gave up pirating when he lost his boon companion, Captain Swann—"

"*Boon companion?* Does that mean what I think it does?"

"Probably not. It means close friend. Was Rufus Blackwell gay? It's possible. There are coeval references to his dandified appearance and his unwholesome and degenerate appetites, which I suppose could be code. There's no question there was a curse, but we don't know the details of it. The mortality rate for children and women in childbirth was very high back then. In fact, the mortality rate in general was very high."

"True." Ellery considered. "Is there any connection between the Blackwells and the Salty Dog?"

Nora looked surprised. "Not that I'm aware of."

"The Blackwells didn't own the pub at one time?"

"No."

"Does the Salty Dog figure into any local legends or ghost stories?"

Nora pursed her lips. "The only ghost story about the Salty Dog that I'm aware of is the 1774 poisoning of a particularly pesky commissioner of customs."

"*Poisoning?*"

"Yes. The pub was called the Black Dog in those days, and it was owned by a rather unsavory tap keeper by the name of Magnus MacGilroy. No relation to the Tulleys."

"Glad to hear it!"

"This exciseman got too nosy about the tunnels leading from the harbor, and, so the story goes, Magnus poisoned him and buried him in his cellar. The cellar is where the ghost is said to make its appearance."

Ellery said thoughtfully, "That's a good way to keep people out of your cellar."

"It is, isn't it?"

When Ellery had finished sorting—i.e., rejecting—most of that morning's new batch of job applications, he phoned Jack.

"I was just thinking about you," Jack said by way of greeting.

"Good things, I hope?" Ellery was smiling.

Jack's chuckle was a little wicked. He didn't comment.

Ellery said, "I called to see if you wanted to go on a stakeout with me?"

There was a pause. Jack said, "As dating options go…"

"I know. But I *think* our prowler is getting into the Salty Dog through the tunnels."

"I thought you said the entrance from the Salty Dog to the tunnels was blocked off."

"I did. The kitchen entrance is blocked off, but I'm wondering if there's another entrance through the cellar. An entrance that maybe Libby and Tom don't know about."

"How would that be possible?"

"I don't know that it is. But he's got to be getting in somehow, and I think I've exhausted the other options." He quoted, "'When you have eliminated the impossible'—"

Jack finished, "'Whatever remains, however improbable, must be the truth.' Thank you, Mr. Holmes. I remember."

Ellery loved the fact that Jack grew up reading mysteries.

"He stole Libby's meat loaf last night."

"Huh?"

"The prowler. He was back last night, and he stole Libby's meat loaf. No sign of him on the security cameras, the alarm never went off, and I really can't believe that any of the pub's guests have anything to do with this."

"Hmm." Jack was noncommittal.

"If you think about it, it makes a lot more sense that the tunnels would lead to the cellar, seeing that the point of the tunnels was largely to smuggle rum and brandy and wine."

"True."

"The cellar at the Salty Dog is supposed to be haunted by the ghost of a murdered exciseman, which to me sounds like an attempt to discourage people poking around the cellar."

"That's not bad," Jack said thoughtfully. "Although I don't understand why there would be two tunnel entrances to the Salty Dog."

"Me neither, and I could be wrong. But I'm running out of ideas."

He waited while Jack thought it over. After a moment, Jack said, "Okay. I'll keep you company tonight. It's not like I have a better idea."

Ellery teased, "Or a better offer?"

He could hear the smile in Jack's, "I definitely don't have a better offer."

CHAPTER THIRTEEN

Ellery's first interview Thursday morning was with a bright and bouncy forty-something brunette by the name of Naomi Puckett.

Naomi began their interview by informing him that the sales floor layout of the Crow's Nest was all wrong. Too many shelves! Too many books! Too confusing for customers! She advised trashing the *gloomy, old-fashioned* paintings and Riker display cases, the (delicate shudder here) *kitschy, creepy* skeleton, and the *second-hand junk* ships' lanterns.

She promised to draw up a diagram for the updated sales floor as soon as she got home.

"Thank you," Ellery said faintly, conscious of the emphatic silence from beyond his office door. He glanced distractedly at Ms. Puckett's impressive CV, and randomly pulled a question from the list he'd downloaded from the *New York Times* business guide.

"Do you have—I mean, what do you consider your greatest weakness?"

"Weakness?" Ms. Puckett sounded like that did not compute. But she was game. "I *might* be a little *too* dedicated. A little *too* responsible. I *might* be *too* much of a perfectionist." She offered a blinding smile, sharing the joke.

A choked sound came from the sales floor. Which was a relief, because for an instant Ellery feared it escaped from his own throat.

He rose, offered his hand. "Thank you so much, Ms. Puckett. We'll be in touch."

Ken Dahl had traveled all the way from Middletown. He was in his thirties, dressed for the beach in cutoffs and tank top, and seemed vaguely irritated at all the questions.

His previous work experience included construction and graphic design.

Ellery asked, and he was genuinely curious, "Why do you want this job?"

Mr. Dahl's expression was one of weary exasperation. "Honestly, I don't even know what I'm doing here. But in order to get unemployment, you have to go on interviews, so..." He shrugged.

Candidate number...who could recall anymore? Anyway, she made a point of saying she was allergic to dogs.

Watson, curled beneath Ellery's desk, head resting on Ellery's foot, gave one of those human-sounding moans, and it was all Ellery could do to keep a straight face. He thanked her for her time.

The candidate after the lady with allergies had quit his last job after punching his boss.

The candidate after the guy who had committed assault was a bookish, thirtyish, lanky-looking fellow with a ponytail and hipster specs. He knew books, he liked books, he had even once worked in a bookstore, although his last position had been in an art gallery in Newport.

"Why did you leave your last job?" Ellery asked. He wasn't sure he wanted to know, because Dorrance—was that his first or last name?—looked perfect both on paper and in real life.

Dorrance sighed and shook his head. "Women. They can't leave me alone, and I can't leave them alone. I had an affair with my boss's wife."

"**F**elix, are you sure you want to go away to college?" Ellery asked on his way out the door. He was not, tempting though the thought was, planning to jump off the pier. Nope, he was going to deliver Miss Blackwell's books to her on his lunch break.

"I could raise your salary fifty cents. Just say the word."

Felix laughed. "Sorry, boss."

"We just have to find that special person," Nora said staunchly, though Ellery thought she too was shaken by the morning's interviews. "There are any number of qualified people out there."

"Way out there," Ellery agreed. "Out of reach out there."

There was a legitimate problem in that the most qualified applicants needed more hours and more money than Ellery could offer. The candidates he could afford were the candidates he did not want. He also had to take into account any prospective employee's compatibility with coworkers, namely Nora and Watson.

"Now. We've only just started the process."

Ellery groaned. "That's not an encouraging thought." He blocked Watson from following him out the door. "Sorry, buddy. Next time."

The bell chimed behind him.

"**W**hat a sweet boy you are," Miss Blackwell cooed after instructing Ellery to toss the bag of books in the tall cupboard. "But I'm leaving this hellhole today whether that fool of a doctor agrees or not."

She was looking much better that afternoon. There was color in her face, and her eyes were bright and alert. She sounded better too, or at least more like her normal, slightly cantankerous self.

Miss Blackwell pointed imperiously at the chair near the window, and Ellery drew it closer to the bed. "You're not nervous about staying alone?"

"Of course not. I've lived alone in that house for nearly twenty years." Her smile didn't quite reach her eyes. "I'm sorry you had such a dreadful experience—and all on my behalf."

"That's all right. It's not your fault."

"I can't help feeling that it is, a little," she admitted. "Thank heavens Chief Carson arrived when he did." She shuddered. "That cellar is very dangerous. The wiring is faulty, and the supporting structure should have been replaced years ago, but that takes money."

"Yes," agreed Ellery feelingly. He knew from his renovations on Captain's Seat exactly what a money pit these old houses could be.

"Did Chief Carson go into the cellar as well?"

"I don't think so. I don't know why he would."

"The staircase is very unsafe. I never go down there."

Ellery nodded absently. He knew from Nora that the Blackwell estate had been mortgaged several times over by Edgar Blackwell, so it was unclear what equity might be left. Property values had jumped like crazy in the last decade. It was an extremely valuable piece of property, made more valuable by the fact that the island's large historic homes rarely, if ever, came on the market. It was common knowledge that Miss Blackwell would not even consider offers to purchase the Black House.

There were probably more easily liquidated assets within the house, but those items might have sentimental value for Miss Blackwell.

She was saying, "Something has to be done about these young hooligans. Chief Carson really ought to make that his priority."

"This wasn't a young hooligan," Ellery said. "This was a grown man dressed like a professional thief."

She seemed to go very still. Her dark eyes never left his face. "Wasn't he? Was he? Did you— Were you able to get a good look at him?"

"Not a good look, no. But I did get enough of a look to know he wasn't any kid. He was older than me. Probably in his forties."

She said nothing.

"Tall, well-built, light hair, high cheekbones, blue eyes..." Ellery watched her carefully.

At the end of his recital, she blinked. "You did get a look at him."

"Yes. Does he sound at all familiar?"

Her thin brows arched. "Familiar? To *me*? No, of course not."

"You don't think maybe he was the person you saw the morning you fainted?"

Her lips parted. She said feebly, "What do mean, my dear? Of course I didn't recognize him. I didn't *see* him. I told you exactly what happened that morning."

"Not really," Ellery said. "Even if I believed that *you* believed you saw the ghost of Rufus Blackwell, your story doesn't really make sense."

He was trying to keep his tone gentle and non-threatening, but she sat back against the pillows, looking affronted.

"What on earth are you getting at, Ellery?" she said in a very different voice.

"Is it possible someone might want to hurt you, Miss Blackwell?"

"Hurt *me*? Of course not. What a...what a strange idea." She looked angry and alarmed. "Why would you suggest such a thing?"

"It's only that I can't understand what your intruder is after."

"The same thing any intruder is after!"

"Money, jewelry, valuables."

She insisted, "Of course."

It was possible the intruder had taken money, jewelry, and valuables. Just because Ellery hadn't seen signs of burglary didn't mean a burglary wasn't in progress. Or was *about* to be in progress. He was speculating, and his speculations were based on very little actual evidence.

"When I entered the house, he was eating jam and cottage cheese."

The color in her face drained away. Her lips moved, but she didn't speak.

"Does that sound like anyone you know?"

She swallowed, shook her head. "No." Her voice was husky. "He made himself at home, didn't he?"

Ellery nodded. "He wasn't expecting to be interrupted."

She stared out the window for a moment or two. Points of color returned to her face. She looked at

Ellery, and there was a dangerous glitter in her eyes as she said softly, "He might be in for a surprise next time."

His scalp prickled in alarm. "If you know who the intruder is, you've *got* to tell Chief Carson."

She snapped, "How many times must I repeat myself? I don't know who this person is!"

She was lying. At the very least, she suspected who the intruder was. Ellery was positive of that. But why? Why on earth would she want to conceal the identity of the person breaking into her home? Why would she want to protect this person? It didn't make sense.

Unless...

Could he be related to her?

Could he be the *jackanapes* boyfriend who disappeared twenty years ago?

Could he be the offspring of that union?

Could he be a nephew? A distant cousin?

Was there a polite way to ask? A way that wouldn't further antagonize her?

If so, Ellery couldn't think of one.

He said slowly, "I don't mean to frighten you, but I think he was there the morning you had your accident."

She did not look frightened. She looked irritated. "I tell you, it was the ghost of Rufus Blackwell that I saw. I could hardly be mistaken."

My point exactly.

But he was getting nowhere with this line of questioning. Ellery shrugged. "Okay. You saw the ghost of Rufus Blackwell."

She continued to watch him with hard, suspicious eyes. Ellery said, "Chief Carson couldn't figure out how the intruder got in. Do you have any ideas?"

"How should I know? The chief must have overlooked something."

"Do you think he could be using the old tunnel system?"

"The old... No." She gave a little shake of her head. "There was a tunnel at one time, but it flooded and collapsed during the Great New England hurricane of 1938. There is no secret passage leading to my home."

That was the first thing she'd said that sounded like the complete and unvarnished truth.

Ellery rose. "I should be getting back to the bookshop. I'm glad you're feeling better."

She relaxed against the pillows. "Thank you, my dear. You must come and visit me once I'm home again."

"Is there anyone who could stay with you until this guy is caught? Any family close by?"

"I have no family left." Her tone was flat and final. But then she summoned a coquettish smile. "But if *you're* offering?"

"Ha, ha, ha," Ellery responded uncomfortably.

Miss Blackwell kept smiling that odd smile. "You're such a charming boy," she murmured. "But you really must keep that handsome nose of yours out of other people's business."

CHAPTER FOURTEEN

"That sounds like a threat!" Nora said when Ellery related his peculiar interview with Miss Blackwell. For the record, Nora did not find the idea of a threat worrying. Her eyes shone with excitement.

"I don't know that it was a threat," Ellery cautioned. "Miss Blackwell doesn't like people meddling in her affairs, and who can blame her."

Nora brushed concern for other people's privacy aside. "One thing we know for sure. She lied about not having family. She has at least one niece in Newport."

"That's right. Cressida's daughter. You mentioned the niece when the Silver Sleuths got together."

"Granted, blood relations don't automatically equal family."

"True."

"Except when it comes to the laws of inheritance." Nora glanced at Ellery. "I don't suppose…"

"I asked her about her will? No." Ellery moved his head in negation. "I'd already offended her plenty without going for the grand slam."

"Did you mention to her that an intruder is also sneaking into the Salty Dog at night?"

"No. I'm pretty sure she'd have denied there was any connection. She's still insisting she saw the ghost of Rufus the morning she was injured."

"Did you suggest the ghost was actually her former companion Robin Mann?"

Ellery's laugh was one of disbelief. "Uh, no. I sure did not. I don't know how you think I could ask her something like that."

"You just put one word in front of the other, dearie."

Ellery shook his head. "She was already making sinister references to my nose. I don't want her to poison my coffee the next time I drop books off."

Nora looked thoughtful. "I suppose poison *would* be her weapon of choice."

"I'd rather not find out firsthand."

"No." Nora's tone was absent.

"What did Mann look like, Nora?"

"A gigolo," she said promptly.

Ellery grinned. "Do tell."

"Tall. Dark hair. Blue eyes. He was very handsome, I'll give you that. A little too slick for my taste. There was something sly in the way he'd look at you."

"*Did* he look at you?" Ellery asked.

Nora nodded curtly. "He looked at every woman. And in the same way. Price per pound."

"Charming."

"He was in it for the money, no mistake. I don't think Juliet was under any illusion. She wanted company and she was willing to pay for it. Up to a point."

"You don't think she loved him?"

Nora said reluctantly, "I suppose it's possible."

"What do you think happened?"

"At a guess? He overplayed his hand. Maybe he forged a check. Maybe he stole money. Most likely she caught him fooling around."

"But you don't know for sure?"

"No. The only thing I know is one day he was here and the next he was gone."

"Did anyone see him go? Did he talk to anyone before he left?"

Nora's brows drew together. "I don't know. That's a very interesting question." Her eyes lit with interest. "Are you suggesting Juliet murdered him? Could it be the ghost of Robin Mann haunting her?"

"What? First of all, I don't believe any *ghost* is haunting her."

"Perhaps it's her guilty conscience."

"I think we're *maybe* getting off the track here."

"Perhaps." Nora sounded regretful. "Come to think of it, it might not be Mann himself. It might be his son. Or a brother. Or another family member hoping to cash in."

"I thought I was confused before. You're saying Miss Blackwell and Robin Mann *did* have a son together?"

"No. I... Well, I suppose it's possible." Nora considered this theory, then shook her head. "It seems unlikely. Not impossible, but unlikely. Juliet was in her sixties. And had there been a child, she would hardly hand it over to *him*. No, I assume he moved on to the next pigeon."

Ellery raised his brows.

"It's the usual chain of events, dearie."

"Is it? Here's the part I still don't understand. If Mann is behind this so-called haunting, what's his motive? Revenge?"

"I think the Robin Manns of this world are more practical than that. The desire for revenge springs from an excess of emotion. My impression was Robin Mann was about as emotional as a calculator.'"

"Then what would be his motive? Would she have put him in her will? Even if she did, would she *leave* him in her will?"

"Perhaps. Depending on the circumstances of their parting?"

"Okay, but according to what everyone knows, their parting amounted to her kicking him out. Here's another thing. If this intruder *is* Miss Blackwell's former gentleman caller, why wouldn't she say so? Why would she pretend she doesn't know who's...haunting her?"

"Now that's a very interesting question. Why *would* she protect him?"

"Isn't a family member a more likely suspect?"

"If true crime writers are to be believed," Nora said dismissively.

"Cressida must have been pretty ruthless to run off with her sister's fiancé. Maybe her daughter inherited that ruthless streak."

"But László Jeles was a very wealthy man. Much richer than the Blackwells. Why would any child of theirs be after Miss Blackwell's estate?"

Ellery shook his head. "We'd have to know more about all of them before we could speculate on motive."

Not that not knowing anything had ever stopped them before.

For a moment they watched Watson doing his best impersonation of a mime, as he tried unsuccessfully to catch a fly buzzing in the corner window. Outside, people passing by the shop, stopped to tap the windows or take cell phone videos.

Hopefully Watson would not go viral.

Ellery said, "Maybe she really *doesn't* know who he is. Maybe she didn't recognize him that morning."

Nora half closed her eyes, thinking. "Robin Mann would have changed in twenty years. He's probably heavier, grayer, more lined. Or, you could be right, maybe this person *isn't* known to her. Maybe he's been hired by someone to arrange a fatal accident. *Or* frighten her to death."

"She seems a long way from being frightened to death." Ellery said slowly, "Or is she?"

"Is she what?"

"Maybe we've got it backward. Maybe Miss Blackwell isn't protecting Robin Mann or anyone else. Maybe Miss Blackwell is protecting *herself*."

Nora looked intrigued. "From what?"

Ellery sighed. "I don't know."

Nora's eyes sparkled. "Then that's exactly what we have to find out."

Ellery was setting up the next day's interviews when Nora popped her head into his office.

"Juliet Blackwell was just delivered to her front doorstep by taxi."

"She's been released from the hospital?"

Nora nodded grimly.

"Well, she did say she wasn't going to spend another night there." Despite his words, Ellery felt uneasy. But it wasn't as though Miss Blackwell didn't understand the potential risk. Not only was she not asking for help, she seemed to resent the very offer.

"I'll let Jack know. Maybe he can have a patrol car swing by during the night just to make sure nothing's amiss."

"That's a good idea."

Miss Blackwell would probably disagree.

Nora added, "I found Wendy Parrish's phone number."

"Who?" The results of Ellery's afternoon job interviews had been no more encouraging than the morning's, so he was thinking this was a potential job candidate.

"Miss Blackwell's niece in Newport."

"*Oh.*"

"Wendy might like to know that her auntie hasn't been well."

Ellery eyed Nora skeptically. "How come I get roped into making all these mission of mercy visits and calls? You'd be much better at it than me."

"Nonsense. Everyone enjoys speaking to a handsome, personable young man."

"How is my handsomeness a factor over the phone?"

Nora said breezily, "You *sound* handsome, dearie. You have a very nice speaking voice. And think how lovely if you were instrumental in bringing about a family reconciliation."

Ellery snorted but took the slip of paper Nora dangled in front of him. "You know the road to hell is paved with good intentions."

She headed for the door, throwing over her shoulder, "I've always thought that was a very cynical attitude."

When Ellery finished speaking to Kingston Peabody, who would be his first and most promising interviewee for Friday, he tried the number on the paper

Nora had handed him and got Wendy Parrish's answering machine.

Not having siblings had given Ellery a slightly sentimental view on the topic of brothers and sisters. He found it sad that Miss Blackwell and her sister had never managed to reconcile, especially given how alone in the world Miss Blackwell seemed.

They said that time healed all wounds, but apparently not.

He was still trying to decide whether he would leave a message when the machine clicked on, and he ended up blurting, "Ms. Parrish, my name is Ellery Page. I'm a sort of a friend of your aunt Juliet. She was recently released from the hospital, and I'm a little concerned for her well-being." He left his cell phone number and hung up.

He hoped that didn't sound too doom and gloomy. He'd never thought of himself as someone prone to butt into other people's business, but in recent months he seemed to be making a career of it. Or at least a sideline.

On impulse, he opened his laptop and tried typing in the name Robin Mann.

Ellery blinked. Within 0.56 seconds Google had returned 53,800,000 results.

Terrific. Now all he needed was a couple of weeks and a small team of investigators to check all these potential suspects out. LinkedIn alone had 400+ *Robin Mann* profiles.

He was frowning over this revelation when Nora startled him by attempting to transfer a call. "Dr. Robert Mane," she said crisply, and promptly disconnected Mane.

It took Ellery a couple of minutes to track Dr. Mane down at his med-center office, and when he finally heard Mane's brisk, "Mane here," he was feeling a peculiar mix of anxiety and anticipation.

"Hey, sorry about that. We're still getting used to our new phone system."

Actually, it was their old phone system, but that just made it worse.

Mane laughed. He had a very nice laugh. "Don't worry. I wasn't giving up that easily."

"I just heard Miss Blackwell was released."

"Yes. She checked herself out against medical advice. But that's not why I'm calling." Mane's tone altered ever so slightly as he said, "I wondered if you'd like to grab dinner tomorrow night?"

"*Dinner?*" Ellery sounded like that was some obscure practice known only to the indoctrinated few.

He could hear the smile in Mane's voice as he said, "Typically the main meal of the day, taken around noontime or, in this case, the evening."

Ellery was smiling too, but he was definitely surprised. "Thank you. The thing is, I'm seeing someone."

"Police Chief Carson," agreed Mane. "I figured."

"You did?"

Mane sounded wry. "I can't remember Carson spending a night sitting beside any other patient's bedside."

"Did he?"

"It doesn't have to be a date," Mane said. "I'd like to know you better. There aren't a lot of...like-minded people in Pirate's Cove."

Like-minded being a new euphemism for gay?

Ellery knew how Mane felt because he'd felt the same when he'd moved to Pirate's Cove. He liked Mane. He'd like to know Mane better. He found him attractive too. Which was why he needed to be cautious. He didn't want to send mixed signals or mess things up with Jack.

He said awkwardly—because there was no graceful way to say it, "Honestly, I'd have to run it by Jack. I don't know what his expectations are."

"That's a good sign," Mane said, and Ellery couldn't help laughing.

"Can I get back to you tomorrow?"

"I'll be disappointed if you don't."

It was light and easy and Ellery was still smiling when he hung up.

True to her word, Nora brought in her copy of *Ghosts of Buck Island*, and after the bookshop closed for the day, Ellery spent an enjoyably alarming few hours reading up on local spooks and specters. He learned, among other things, that the Crow's Nest had once been a tavern known as the Sea Horse, and, sure enough, had its own ghostly legend, which sounded suspiciously like the seafaring version of a poem he'd read in high school called "The Highwayman."

But the tale that interested him most was naturally that of Rufus Blackwell. Nora had pretty much covered the basics, but there was a not very good ink drawing of Rufus, noose around his neck and midspeech on the gallows. He was decked out in full pirate costume: knee breeches, fancy shirt, jerkin, sash, buckle shoes, and tricorn hat with plume. Was that an actual likeness of Rufus? Was that an actual likeness of anybody? Also, would they really let him wear that hat to be hanged?

Anyway, it did seem that Rufus had no sooner had his neck stretched than he'd popped back over to Buck Island and proceeded to terrify the natives at every opportunity.

Whether the ghost of Rufus Blackwell was real seemed almost immaterial, given how many different reports of Rufus sightings there were. People *believed* in the ghost of Rufus—the Blackwells appeared to believe in the ghost of Rufus—and wasn't that what really mattered?

It was after midnight when Jack's SUV pulled up silently in front of the Crow's Nest.

Ellery locked the front door and led Watson to the SUV. He scooped Watson up, opened the rear passenger door, and greeted Jack.

Jack looked from Ellery to Watson. "You're kidding. You're bringing Watson on stakeout?"

"I wasn't going to," Ellery said apologetically. "I arranged with Terry next door to puppysit, but I figured it'll be so late by the time we get out of there, and I hate to leave him overnight. He seems to be suffering from separation anxiety lately."

Watson looked from Ellery to Jack, eyes shining, tail wagging hopefully.

"Are you sure *he's* the one suffering separation anxiety?" Jack asked.

"Well…"

Jack sighed, shook his head, but made no further objections as Ellery hooked the seat belt through Watson's safety harness.

As they pulled away from the Crow's Nest, Ellery said, "Thanks for doing this, Jack. I know it's kind of an ask."

No lie. One thing Ellery had learned in recent weeks was that Jack was a guy who needed his sleep. He burned a lot of energy, both physical and nervous, and he was not much for late nights.

"If I'm going to lose sleep over you, I might as well be with you when I do it." Jack's tone was rueful.

"I don't really think there's any danger involved in this. I can't imagine Libby's prowler will show up two nights in a row. He never has before."

"Yeah, well, I admit you've got me curious about whether there's a way into the tunnels from the Salty Dog's cellar."

"And I promise if tonight doesn't pan out—or even if it does—I'll talk to Tom myself."

"That would be a good idea." That was Jack's no-nonsense tone. He was very much a by-the-rules kind of guy. In fact, the first time they'd met, Jack had written Ellery a warning for a ceiling vent violation in the Crow's Nest customer restroom.

They parked one street over from the Salty Dog, cut through the long alley, and then walked down to the pub, Watson stopping to sniff every flowerpot, lamppost, and bicycle rack.

The shops' windows were dark, the streets almost eerily quiet after the buzz and bustle of another jam-packed summer day. The night felt refreshingly cool and humid, though the daytime scents of fried foods and suntan oil and gasoline still seemed to linger in the air. Overhead, the stars appeared tiny and faraway, glittering sea anemones awash in seafoam clouds.

Ellery said, "I've been thinking."

"That's what I like about you."

"And I have an idea about how Miss Blackwell's intruder could be getting into her house without using a secret passage or leaving any sign of a break-in."

"How's that?" Jack asked.

"He could have a key."

Jack seemed to miss a step. He stopped walking and stared. "He could have a *key*?"

"If the intruder is Robin Mann, Miss Blackwell's former companion, he probably had a key. Who's to say he didn't hang on to it? And given what I know of Miss Blackwell, well, not just Miss Blackwell, pretty much everyone around here, what are the odds she changed the locks after he left? I saw that keyring of hers. I'd bet money the locks haven't been changed at the Black House since the 1950s."

"That's a bet I don't want to take." Jack said he'd do some checking into what Mr. Mann might be doing these days, but added, "You do know that it's pretty unlikely someone would wait twenty years to seek revenge for being dumped, right?"

"Sure, but it wouldn't just be about getting revenge. There could be a monetary angle. He could be in her will."

"God help him. I hope he likes broken clocks and dreary paintings."

Ellery chuckled. "I know, but the property itself could be worth a fortune."

"It would certainly take a fortune to make that place livable."

"But what if that's not the goal? What if the plan is to raze the house to the ground and build a nice big condominium in its place? Between island property values and the housing shortage…"

Jack looked thoughtful, but said only, "I'll look into it."

They reached the Salty Dog at last. Upstairs and downstairs, the windows were all dark. The old-fashioned green and white sign rocked gently in the night breeze.

"Do you think there's a family resemblance to Watson?" Ellery gazed up at the painted grinning dog. "Something about the nose and the ears?"

Jack considered. "Something about the way he balances a beer mug on his head?"

Ellery was chuckling as he handed Watson's leash to Jack and unlocked the door. He pushed the door open. It took his eyes a moment to adjust to the dark.

He said softly, "The keypad is over to the right..."

Out of the corner of his eye, Ellery caught a flicker of motion. He turned, and his heart jumped in alarm at the sight of glowing red coals in the fireplace and two shadows seeming to rise out of nowhere.

Watson also jumped in alarm—and began to bark.

Arf. Arf. Arf.

"Police! Show yourself!" Jack's voice was hard and unfamiliar.

"*E-E-Ellery?*" squeaked Libby.

"It's us, Chief," Felix called. His voice wobbled. "Don't shoot."

Shoot?

Ellery glanced around and was shocked to see that, yes, Jack had dropped Watson's leash—he had one boot firmly planted on it—and had drawn his weapon. Even as Ellery absorbed this, Jack was holstering his pistol.

"What in hell's name are you two doing in here?" Jack rapped out in that same harsh stranger's voice.

Ellery understood Jack's anger was actually fear—fear of what might have happened if he hadn't recognized the two youngsters, if he'd misread them for a genuine threat.

Libby and Felix were both stammering incoherent explanations.

Didn't realize.

Wasn't expecting.

Didn't know.

Weren't doing anything wrong.

Arf. Arf. Arf.

"Watson, *stop.*" Ellery picked up Watson, who stopped barking but struggled affrontedly to be put down. "Libby, why are you here? We weren't expecting anyone." He too felt shaken at the idea of how very wrong things could have gone.

Jack reached past him and flipped on the overheads. Ellery winced at the sudden blaze of light.

Two chairs had been pulled up in front of the fireplace. Next to the chairs were two half-empty mugs of beer. Felix and Libby stood shoulder to shoulder. They both looked like they'd been crying.

Libby said, "We just started talking, and I lost track of the time. I was going to call you and tell you not to come. That Felix would watch with me tonight. I just forgot."

"*Forgot?*" Ellery echoed.

Forgot?

Forgot to tell him he didn't have to stay up all night, lurking in an empty pub, instead of going home to his nice comfy bed?

"I'm sorry, Chief," Felix was saying at the same time. "It's my fault. I told Libby I'd keep watch with her tonight. We were trying not to disturb anybody."

Fat chance of that. Once again, lights were going on upstairs. Doors were opening. Voices were calling out.

"What's going on?"

"Who's there?"

"Did you hear that?"

"Is Pepper back?"

"IS THERE NO CHANCE OF GETTING ANY SLEEP IN THIS PLACE?"

Jack swore under his breath, but he was a man who thought fast on his feet.

"Hey, it's your party," he told Libby and Felix. "You two have a good evening."

He pushed open the pub door, hooked his hand around Ellery's arm, and drew him outside.

The door swung shut, cutting off the steady rise of voices, and settled into its frame with a heavy sigh of relief.

CHAPTER FIFTEEN

"**S**he *forgot*?" Ellery repeated in disbelief.

Jack had already moved on. "Plan B," he said.

Ellery let Watson down. Watson shook himself with an air of outrage and lifted his leg to let the management of the Salty Dog know what he thought of their establishment. "*Hey,*" Ellery warned him. To Jack, he said, "Do we *have* a Plan B?"

"Yep. Come on."

Jack's boots pounded the pavement briskly, Watson's tags jingling softly as they headed back the way they'd come through silent, sleeping streets. Overhead, the crescent moon drifted like a ghost ship through the wispy clouds.

"There's another way to verify if the Salty Dog has an entrance to the tunnels," Jack was saying. "We go through the tunnels and check."

"I thought the tunnels were fenced off."

"The known exterior entrances are gated. I have a key."

Ellery stared. "You have a key?"

"I have a key, the mayor, well, acting mayor, has a key, and Zeb Young, the former air-raid warden, had the third key. I'm not sure if the family still has it or not. They say no, but..."

"You never mentioned you had a key to the tunnels."

"You never asked." Jack winked at him.

At that time of night, the drive to Old Harbor took less than three minutes.

Jack parked outside the gated mouth of the cave which served as entrance to the tunnels. Ellery couldn't help thinking that from the outside, the cave looked very much like the entryway to a terrific Disneyland themed area.

Jack turned off the SUV's engine and half turned to face Ellery. "Here's the deal. Watson has to wait here."

Watson, sitting in the back seat, one ear tipped forward, one ear tipped back, heard his name and looked hopefully from Jack to Ellery.

Ellery opened his mouth, but Jack wasn't through. "There's no stealth approach with Watson. I don't know what we're walking into, but I don't want to have to try to protect both you and him."

"You don't have to *protect* me—"

"Again, I don't know what we're walking into." Jack's gaze held Ellery's. "*You* don't know what we're walking into." He was dead serious.

Ellery let out an exasperated breath. "Okay. But he's not going to wait quietly."

"He can bark all he wants from the safety of the SUV. We'll open the windows a crack, and I'll even leave a thermal blanket with him. He'll be perfectly comfortable."

"Tell it to him."

Jack said to Watson, "You'll be perfectly comfortable."

Watson wagged his tail and reverse-ordered his ears.

"I have an extra flashlight if you need it."

"Are you talking to me or Watson?"

Jack grimaced.

Ellery held up his flashlight. "And I have my phone."

"That's another thing. You probably won't be able to get a signal down there."

"Understood."

"Great. Let's go." Jack opened the SUV door.

Watson began to protest before they were halfway to the mouth of the cave. Jack unlocked the formidable-looking key box and noisily shoved aside the gate.

"If someone's getting in and out of the tunnels, they must have another way in," Ellery observed. That gate, which went all the way to the roof of the cave, had not been designed for decorative purposes.

"That's more than possible. I'm not sure if anyone still living has explored the entire network of tunnels."

"Like the catacombs of Paris." Ellery added lightly, "Though hopefully with fewer skulls."

"Hopefully."

Sand whispered beneath their feet as they proceeded into the cave. Their flashlight beams played over the pale sandstone walls. Watson's protests faded.

"I didn't realize the original cave was so large," Ellery said after several yards of rocky stone and slippery sand.

"Yeah," Jack said. "The natural cave formation stretches inland for about two miles. The tunnels branch off and run on for...God only knows."

"I thought maybe you were exaggerating."

"Nope. Not at all. It's not like this was built to code. There was no single architect at work here. And there was no project start or end date. In fact, I've heard theories that families were still adding tunnels right through Prohibition."

"Yikes."

Jack glanced at Ellery, his eyes dark in the glare of the flashlight. "It would be very easy to get lost down here."

Ellery didn't miss the warning. Not necessary. He had no intention or interest in exploring these tunnels on his own. He also understood better Jack's concern about bringing Watson, who had developed a new trick of slipping out of his harness, into the tunnels.

"Got it. So there's no map of the tunnels?"

"We've got a map. Sort of." Jack stopped and drew out what appeared to be a short stack of yellowed paper that, once unfolded, turned out to be a faded copy of a mimeographed handwritten map.

Ellery moved close, his shoulder brushing Jack's. "That doesn't look like the work of the Thomas Brothers."

Jack's mouth curved. "No. This was drawn up during the war by Zeb Young when there were fears of a possible invasion. The government offered to evacuate the island, since it couldn't be effectively defended, but the islanders chose to stay."

"That doesn't surprise me."

"No. Me neither." Jack directed his flashlight beam to the map, the yellow circle of light gliding slowly across the tiny purple-blue letters, lines, and symbols. "You can see the problem. These lines are branches off the main tunnel. The dotted lines are branches off branches. A lot of these branches, maybe most of them, have never been mapped. And just to keep things interesting, some of the original tunnels have caved in or flooded or were deliberately closed off. I think Zeb probably knew these tunnels better than anyone, and he said he'd never explored the entire thing."

"So there could be any number of secret ways into the tunnels?"

The cave acoustics performed like a giant sea-shell, seeming to scoop up and whisper back the echo of waves hitting the harbor outside, sending Ellery's quiet words reverberating down the tunnels.

Secret way...

Secret way...

Secret...

Way...

"Exactly," Jack said. He glanced at Ellery. "Cold?"

"Nah," Ellery lied. It was definitely colder this far into the cave. Cold and damp and dank-smelling. Exciting, of course, but not exactly comfortable.

Jack started to shrug out of his jacket.

"No. Way. I should have thought to bring a jacket."

"You didn't know we were going into the tunnels." Jack handed his jacket over.

"Jack..." But there was no winning this argument. Ellery pulled Jack's police bomber jacket on. "Thanks." He shook his head at Jack, but Jack just smiled.

"You're welcome."

They continued on until they came to a Y in the cave.

Jack said, "The branch to the right leads to a gated storage area for emergency supplies. There's even a small generator."

Ellery nodded.

"Straight ahead we go down a short flight of stone steps, and then we're in the tunnels for real."

"Yay," Ellery murmured.

Jack laughed. "Sorry you came?"

"No. Definitely not sorry."

Jack's look was approving.

They went down the sandy steps, and Ellery was startled to find they had reached a large central area with a series of brick arched doorways leading off in all directions.

Jack consulted his map and pointed to the western archway. "The Salty Dog is in that direction."

Their feet thudded on the hard-packed ground. The ceiling of the tunnel was claustrophobically lower than in the cave section. Unseen things scuttled in the shadows, disappearing into crumbling patches of brickwork.

Ellery was starting to feel like they'd spent half their lives marching through the clammy darkness when Jack stopped abruptly.

"I think that's it." His flashlight beam traveled up a short flight of steps to a round door with an iron ring for a handle.

"It's so small," Ellery said. "I was looking for something taller. Something door-shaped. This is hobbit-sized."

"Barrel-sized," Jack said.

"*Ah.* Right."

They approached the small door, and Ellery noticed there was no lock on it.

Jack put a finger to his lips and pulled open the door. It opened silently on well-oiled hinges. They exchanged looks. There was no mistaking the significance of that.

Jack bent down and went through the door. Ellery followed and discovered that the door seemed to open behind a tall wooden shelf. Jack gently pushed the shelf, which swung silently out, offering them a view of the crowded cellar.

In the partial darkness, he could make out racks of wine bottles, storage casks for beer, metal canisters, crates of bottles, a complicated web of lines and tubes leading through the ceiling to the taps above. The "shelf" covering the doorway into the tunnel was in fact a false wall of very old casks cleverly fastened together to create the illusion that the shelf was much deeper and heavier than it appeared.

For a few moments Jack and Ellery stood motionless in the refrigerated gloom, listening.

Ellery could just make out the soft murmur of voices. Felix and Libby were still talking.

He looked at Jack, who nodded his head toward the tunnel entrance. Ellery turned and retraced his footsteps, exiting the way they'd come.

They eased shut the round door behind them, went down the steps.

"That's how he's getting in," Ellery said.

"Yes."

"And that's how he's able to move from the cellar to the kitchen and back, and never be seen on camera."

"Or trigger the alarm."

"But how is he getting into the tunnels to start with? And how would he know he could get into the Salty Dog this way?"

"He's no stranger to the area," Jack said. "He knows his history. In fact, he knows his history better than half the people currently living in the village."

That was a troubling thought. Ellery had been assuming, hoping, the prowler was a summer visitor. But this familiarity with the tunnels did not indicate a tourist. Quite the opposite.

Jack was already moving off toward another one of the archways. Ellery followed.

He wasn't sure what they were looking for, but Jack seemed to have something in mind, and several yards down, they found a folded stack of army blankets, the empty bottle of Woodford Reserve Double Oaked Bourbon, and the meat-loaf tin.

Jack pulled on blue nitrile gloves, drew out an evidence bag, and gingerly placed the bottle inside the bag.

"You think there'll be fingerprints?" Ellery asked.

"I do, yeah. He wasn't expecting company."

"But what's he doing living down here in the first place?"

Jack shook his head. "He can't afford to be seen."

"Yet? Or at all?"

"You tell me."

Ellery doubtfully shone his flashlight around the empty space, swinging the light back abruptly at the sight of what, for a terrifying instant, he mistook for a figure standing there.

"Hey, Jack. Look at this." He moved closer for a better look.

Jack came to join him. For a long moment they studied the garments hanging neatly from a hanger hooked over a jutting rock.

Not just any garments. Brown knee breeches, a white fancy shirt, fawn-colored jerkin, scarlet sash, and, sitting tidily on a pair of black buckle shoes, a tricorn hat with a green plume.

"You've got to be kidding me," Jack muttered.

"No," Ellery said. "Meet the ghost of Rufus Blackwell."

CHAPTER SIXTEEN

"**W**hat's worrying me is if he's not in the tunnels and he's not at the Salty Dog, where *is* he?" Ellery said.

They were sitting in the SUV outside the gated tunnel entrance. Ellery was stroking Watson, who'd had a thing or two to say about being left alone AGAIN in a dark car in an unfamiliar place. Jack absently drummed his fingers on the steering wheel, staring out at the shuttered boats in the harbor.

"He's not at Miss Blackwell's. Not without his ghost pirate costume. What would be the point?"

"True."

Jack said, "Maybe he cleared out?"

"You think?"

"Maybe he achieved what he set out to do."

Ellery said, "Which was what? Scare an old lady?"

"Maybe he found what he was looking for."

"*If* he was looking for anything." At Jack's questioning look, Ellery said, "What if he wasn't trying to steal something. What if he was trying to *plant* something?"

"Like what?"

"A birth certificate, a deed to her property, a will, a murder weapon…"

Jack repeated, "A murder weapon?"

"Just throwing ideas out there."

Jack grunted.

Ellery considered, sighed. "It turns out Miss Blackwell wasn't lying. She did see the ghost of Rufus Blackwell."

"That doesn't mean she wasn't lying." Jack spoke with the brisk cynicism of years in law enforcement. "It just means she wasn't lying about everything."

"You think she knows who Rufus's ghost really is?"

"What do you think?"

Ellery said, "I think she knows. If the intruder is Robin Mann, she'd have to know. Even if he looks different now. Even if he changed his appearance."

Jack nodded. "Probably. But if that's the case, the question becomes, why would she keep that information to herself? Why would she protect him?"

"Yeah, that I can't figure out. She's more afraid of the truth coming out than she is of whoever is trying to scare her. Only he's not just trying to scare her, because what's there to gain from that? He's…"

"He's trying to kill her." Jack was matter-of-fact.

Ellery stared at him.

Jack smiled without humor. "He can't inherit if she's not dead. He's trying to scare her to death. Right?"

"Well… Right. So who is he?"

"You probably have a better idea than I do. You've been working this case for a week."

For an instant, Ellery was taken aback, but actually, Jack *was* right. One way or another, Ellery had been trying to unravel Miss Blackwell's predicament for the past week.

"I keep coming back to Robin Mann."

"The boyfriend."

"Right."

"Because he *might* still be in her will?"

"I know it sounds flimsy."

"That's never stopped you before."

"Ha. Well, Mann might have a motive. That's the first thing. Granted, it's the same motive her remaining family members might have."

"Financial gain."

"Right. He could be in her will. The less flimsy part is he's someone Miss Blackwell would surely recognize. Mann would have had a key to the Black House. Maybe he held on to it. He would know the house, he would know the island, he would know about the tunnels, and he might know of an alternative way into the tunnels."

"That's a lot of might and maybe."

"I know."

Jack continued to think, continued that restless tattoo of fingers on steering wheel. "As you say, the motive of financial gain holds true for Miss Blackwell's relatives. There's a sister somewhere?"

"The sister may have passed by now. She was older than Miss Blackwell. But there's a niece. Wendy Parrish. She lives in Newport. I left her a message today but didn't hear back."

"If anybody is in Miss Blackwell's will, wouldn't it most likely be her family?"

"Probably. Yes."

Jack sighed, scooted his seat forward, turned the key in the ignition. "We're not going to solve this tonight. Tomorrow I'll have another chat with Miss Blackwell and see if I can persuade her to open up about what's really going on. Did you want me to drop you at the Crow's Nest, or did you want to crash at my place?"

Ellery thought of the dark, lonely drive to Captain's Seat. He shook his head. "If it's okay, I'll crash at your place."

"Of course it's okay." Jack put the SUV in motion.

Though Ellery and Jack had been friends for a few months, they had not been the kind of friends who casually dropped in on each other. In fact, he'd never been to Jack's little beach cottage in the heart of Pirate's Cove.

Watson had, though, and as soon as Jack unlocked the front door and pushed it open, Watson bounded inside, grabbed a green squeezy frog from beneath the coffee table, and proceeded to trot around Ellery and Jack, wringing pitiful squeaks from the frog.

Ellery groaned, but Jack offered a weary grin. "He's okay. Do you need anything?"

"Sleep," Ellery said.

"I was going to make a hot drink—"

"A hot drink and sleep," Ellery amended.

Jack nodded at the tailored blue sofa. "Make yourself comfortable." He headed toward the door leading into the kitchen. "I think I have an unopened toothbrush somewhere."

Ellery dropped down on the sofa. The living room—well, everything from the immaculate front garden to this room and beyond—was almost intimidatingly tidy. It was a pleasant room with large windows offering a nice view of the pretty yard and quaint street. The furniture looked comfortable, and the furnishings were coordinated in restful shades of blue. There were no pictures on the wall, no books anywhere, no framed photographs or knickknacks or souvenirs.

It looked like a model home. In every sense.

Watson zoomed past the sofa, green froggy still shrieking for mercy, and disappeared into the kitchen.

"Hey, you rascal." Jack sounded tired.

In a way, Ellery was not surprised by how... *Sterile* was not the right word. Pristine? Spotless? Unlived in? Jack's home was. Jack didn't spend a lot of time in his cottage. He was up early, worked late, and could usually be found at the police station. He was careful and conscientious, so all this daunting cleanliness was only to be expected. But he was also warm and considerate and generous, so in that way, the lack of anything particularly personal or revealing in the house did surprise him.

It was funny. Sometimes he felt like he'd known Jack forever. But in other ways, Jack was still very much an unknown quantity.

Jack, accompanied by Watson and his talking frog, reappeared in the living room, carrying two red mugs. He handed one cup of milky hot liquid to Ellery and sat beside him on the sofa.

Ellery sniffed the mug. "What is it?"

"Ovaltine." Jack smiled at Ellery's expression. "Hannah used to like a cup before bed."

Ellery smiled back. "I haven't had Ovaltine in a million years."

Hannah had been Jack's wife, and she'd been carrying Jack's child when she died in a traffic accident. That was before Jack moved to Buck Island to become Pirate Cove's police chief. Hannah was one example of the occasional failings of the island's information network. According to gossip, Hannah and Jack had been childhood sweethearts, and Hannah had died in a hit-and-run. In fact, they had been college sweethearts, and the driver, who'd been texting when he should have been watching the road, had been caught and prosecuted to the fullest extent of the law. For all the comfort that provided.

Ellery sipped his Ovaltine. The vaguely malted-chocolate flavor wasn't bad. It was even sort of soothing. Watson loped past again, frog squealing, apparently hoping to lure them into his favorite game of chase.

"If she left him in her will, she must have feelings for him," Ellery said.

Jack, still cradling his mug of Ovaltine, had leaned back and closed his eyes. He opened his eyes. "You don't know that she left him in her will. That's pure speculation. Personally, I think it's unlikely she'd throw him out but leave him in her will."

It did seem unlikely.

"Maybe he's not looking for her will. Maybe he's looking for something else."

"Her lawyer will have her will."

"Will he, though? I wonder. Miss Blackwell is kind of..."

"Irascible." Jack sat up. "Idiosyncratic." He drained his mug.

"Yes. She seems like the type who wouldn't trust lawyers and would keep her life savings beneath her mattress."

"Maybe that's what he's looking for. Her life savings."

"Maybe. In which case, he probably got what he was after." Somehow, Ellery didn't think that was the case. He said absently, "He might not know she checked herself out of the hospital." Ellery finished his Ovaltine. He was thinking of how Miss Blackwell kept referring to Robert Mane as *that fool doctor*.

Which reminded him...

He glanced at Jack. "This is off the subject, but...are we exclusive?"

Jack looked blank. "Exclusive?"

"When it comes to dating, I mean."

It seemed it *was* kind of a funny question because Jack had a funny look on his face. "I..."

Don't have an answer.

Clearly.

Ellery hadn't been thinking this was liable to be painful. One minute earlier, he'd been feeling secure in his relationship with Jack—or at least feeling secure that they were both on the same page as far as their relationship.

Now it seemed like maybe not?

He said hastily, "I'm not pressuring you. I'm only bringing it up because Robert Mane asked me to dinner, and I told him we were going out." He added doubtfully, "I hope that's okay?"

"Of course it's okay," Jack said curtly. "It's also okay if you want to go to dinner with Mane."

Was that supposed to be reassuring? It was not remotely reassuring.

"Right," Ellery said vaguely. "Okay."

They were both silent. It was not their normal, comfortable silence.

Finally, Ellery said, "I feel like you're—"

At the same instant, Jack said, "Ellery—"

They both jerked to a stop.

"Go on," Jack said.

"No, sorry. What did you want to say?"

Jack blurted, "Honestly, I wasn't thinking that far ahead. I've been taking it one day at a time, and so far, all the days are good. Great, even. I like being with you. I want to spend more time with you. I want to meet your parents."

"But?"

"I don't think there's a but in there. I guess I'm just not ready to— It didn't occur to me that—"

That was easy to translate. Jack wasn't ready to make a commitment, and it hadn't occurred to him that anyone else was going to ask Ellery out.

Ellery's smile was twisted. "It's okay, Jack. I'm not looking for a marriage proposal."

"I *know* you're not," Jack said quickly, sincerely. "And the truth is, I'll be jealous as hell if you go out with Mane. I don't like that idea. At all. But I also know it's not fair to demand exclusivity when I'm not ready to make or ask for a commitment."

Ellery nodded. His heart felt heavy, which wasn't reasonable. Jack wasn't saying anything he hadn't already sensed. Ellery wasn't looking for a commitment from Jack either. But he did feel that, the way things were going, they were maybe headed that way eventually.

Or at least that's how he'd felt before they talked. Instead of clearing the air, he felt this conversation had clouded the situation.

Jack's gaze seemed to search his face for...what?

"I care for you," Jack said. "I don't want to do anything to damage...us. I'm not interested in seeing anyone else. But if you are, that's okay. I'm not going to be a jerk about it."

"I appreciate the honesty."

"Do you?" Jack asked. "Because I feel like there's a wall between us that wasn't there a minute ago."

It was a relief to know Jack was feeling that same uncertainty, that same concern that instead of bringing them closer, his honesty had driven a wedge between them. Jack was saying the right things, doing the right things, and how could that not be enough? It was *more* than enough, given what a short time they'd known each other.

Ellery smiled, and this time he meant it. "Jack, we've been dating for...what? Not even three weeks. I feel the same. I don't want to jeopardize *us*, but I'm not ready to make any commitments either. The only reason I felt like I should bring this up is Pirate's Cove is a fishbowl. Everybody sees everything and has an opinion on everything. So I just wanted to be sure we both have the same understanding."

"I want and intend to pursue this relationship," Jack said.

"Same. If I go out with Robert, it'll be as friends."

Jack's smile was lopsided. "You and I started out as friends. So that's not going to make me feel a whole lot happier about it, but that's my problem, not yours."

"Well, yeah," Ellery agreed, but he was smiling.

Jack could not cook.

"I'm glad I discovered your fatal flaw now," Ellery said, unplugging the smoking toaster and fishing out the charred remnants of what had once been an English muffin. "I don't even want to know what's in that pan."

"Just eggs," Jack assured him, with a quick, uneasy glance at the congealed mess on the stove. "And ham."

"*Hamartia* and eggs," Ellery said, which was an old theater joke. Waking up with Jack had been very nice, and he was in a good mood. He glanced again at the pan and did a double take. "Is that—*was that*—*lunchmeat*?"

"Kind of the same thing?" Jack suggested.

"Jack, that's pimento loaf. It's not the same thing." Ellery said admiringly, "You really *can't* cook."

"Hey, I'm great at making sandwiches."

"Not if you're using pimento loaf, you're not." Ellery grinned. "I didn't realize there were any of you left. I feel like I'm in the presence of a significant archeological find."

So yes, maybe they were being extra jokey, extra playful, extra extra. Ellery felt like they'd narrowly skirted disaster the night before but managed to come through safely. He was relieved and happy.

Watson, gulping down canned puppy food like it was crack cocaine, wagged his tail at their nonsense but never looked up.

When Jack's cell phone rang, he threw Ellery a look of apology and took the call. "Carson."

There was something odd about the silence that followed. Ellery, investigating the fridge for break-fast alternatives, glanced around and was surprised by Jack's stony expression.

"When?" Jack's voice was flat.

Silence.

"Who discovered the body?"

Silence.

"I'll be there in five." Jack clicked off. He met Ellery's gaze. "Grab your stuff. I'll drop you off at the Crow's Nest."

"What happened? What's wrong?"

"Miss Blackwell's dead. Her cleaning lady found her a little while ago at the bottom of her staircase."

CHAPTER SEVENTEEN

Unsurprisingly, Nora had already heard the sad news of Miss Blackwell's demise when she arrived at the Crow's Nest shortly after Ellery.

"I'm calling an emergency meeting of the Silver Sleuths tonight," she informed him by way of greeting, and by the time Ellery had a response, she was already on the phone.

"Nora, hold on," Ellery protested. "This is a police matter now."

Nora covered the mouthpiece with her hand. Her tone was kind. "Yes, it is. But you must've noticed the police aren't exactly batting a thousand on this one, dearie."

"Now wait just a minute."

Nora amended, "Not that it's Chief Carson's fault. The police are hamstrung in their investigations in ways that the amateur is not."

The amateur in question could practically feel his hair curling at that remark. "Nora, seriously. It's one thing to poke around and ask a few questions about some mysterious happenings. But a woman is dead."

"*Exactly,*" Nora said. "And it could very well be an accident. But it could very well *not* be an accident."

"But either way, this is now up to the police to investigate."

"*Of course,*" Nora said soothingly, and spoke into the phone. "Hermione? Yes. *Yes.* What else have you heard? *Really?*"

Ellery opted for plausible deniability and retreated to his office.

For once Sue Lewis had been caught napping. Even the online edition of the *Scuttlebutt Weekly* had nothing to report on the passing of one of Pirate Cove's oldest and most notorious citizens.

Ellery was frowning over that anomaly—lack of facts didn't typically stop Sue from coming up with her own version of events—when someone tapped on the office doorframe.

Felix hovered in the doorway, looking sheepish.

Ellery shook his head but beckoned to the chair in front of his desk.

Felix crossed the room and dropped down in the chair. "Man, I'm *so* sorry. It's just once we started talking, we lost track of time, and then you and Chief Carson walked in…"

Felix looked so tired and so happy, it was hard to stay irritated.

"It's fine." Ellery sighed. "Everyone needs a good jolt of adrenaline now and then. So things are okay between you and Libby again?"

"Thing are *great* between me and Libby again."

"I'm glad to hear it. I'm glad something good came out of this, because I promised Jack—Chief Carson—that I'd call Libby's dad and tell him what's been going on the past week. And I may not know Tom well, but I know him well enough to know he's not going to be happy."

Felix winced. "You don't think you could—"

"I sure don't," Ellery said. "I'm in deep enough as it is."

Felix nodded reluctantly, then brightened. "It might be okay, though, because Libby's changed her mind about not going to college."

"You guys really did talk!"

"Yeah. We did. And Mr. Tulley will be happy about that, about her accepting her scholarship."

"I think he will. You never know," Ellery said.

But in fact, Tom *was* delighted by the news that Libby had reversed course and was going away to college as originally planned. So much so that even Ellery's news about what had been happening in the pub during his absence only slightly dented his good mood.

"She did *what*?"

Ellery explained yet again about being hired to investigate the mysterious happenings at the Salty Dog.

"What's she paying you?"

"We never discussed that."

"You never…"

"I wasn't actually going to *charge* her."

Tom made a sound of pure exasperation. "If you had, you could have put an end to the whole thing there and then."

That was probably true. Ellery said, "It turns out she was right. Someone *was* getting into the pub."

Tom said, "That makes not telling me all the worse."

Ellery winced. "I know, and I wanted to, believe me, but Libby was so…shaken up by you being sick. I think she really believed hearing about the prowler was going to be too much for you."

Tom groaned. "That crazy kid."

"Anyway, it turns out the prowler was getting in through a second entrance to the tunnels, which is located in your cellar."

Silence followed Ellery's words.

"*Oh.*" Tom's voice sounded funny.

"Oh?" Ellery repeated. "What does *oh* mean?"

Tom cleared his throat. "It means, there was only ever one entrance to the tunnels. I faked the kitchen wall to look like I'd bricked up a doorway."

"*Why?*"

"I didn't want Libby snooping around, trying to find the real way into the tunnels. I know kids. I know *my* kid. She's just like me, and at her age I was hanging out at Skull House, looking for tunnels. Libby would've thought a secret passage was the coolest thing ever. But this way, she grew up believing the tunnel was closed off."

"I don't get it. Why didn't you close it off for real?"

Tom sounded flabbergasted. "Close off our entrance to the tunnels? Are you kidding me? Those tunnels are good for everything from a bomb shelter to extra storage. No way would I really close off our access to the tunnel system."

"But..."

"Think of the trouble you could have saved yourself if you'd just *asked*," Tom interrupted, and to that there was really no good answer.

"I have to admit, I've never actually worked in a bookstore, but I've always wanted to. I remember the Crow's Nest from my visits to the island many years ago." Kingston Peabody smiled fondly at those distant memories.

He was a small, dapper man of about seventy or so. Behind natty gold-rim spectacles, his eyes were green. His straight silver hair was a little long in the back. He wore high-waisted brown trousers, a white short-sleeved shirt, and a brown bow tie with tiny green polka dots.

Ellery liked Mr. Peabody. He seemed like a character in a play Ellery would write. Watson liked Mr. Peabody too, and had tried twice during the interview to climb into his lap. But educated and affable as Mr. Peabody might be, he was not really what Ellery was looking for. He had been hoping for someone, well, a little younger, a little sturdier. Working in a bookstore meant being on your feet all day. It meant lugging heavy stacks of books around. It meant scaling ladders and crawling around on the floor. Mr. Peabody looked like a hard wind could blow him over. Ellery already had one of those. And though he wouldn't trade Nora for all the brawny thirty-somethings out there, he'd been hoping to find someone to balance the scales.

"Here's the thing," Ellery said apologetically, though he wasn't exactly sure what he was apologizing for. "This is a part-time position and, to be honest, it might not even exist once tourist season is over. It's really quiet here during the winter months."

Mr. Peabody smiled. "I remember very well. It's very peaceful."

"Uh, yes, peaceful is exactly right. The business might not be there to support this position."

"*Ah.*" Mr. Peabody nodded regretfully.

"Also, I notice that you live in Narragansett, so you'd have the expense and hassle of taking the ferry several times a week."

"I see. Yes." Mr. Peabody took out a pristine hanky, removed his spectacles, wiped them, replaced his spectacles, and refolded his hanky. "I don't know if this makes any difference to your decision-making, but I'm planning to move to the island. Which is why your want ad seemed so serendipitous."

"Move *here*?" Ellery said, as though such a thing were unthinkable.

"Yes. As I said, I have such happy memories of past visits. My children are grown now, and my dear wife passed away last year after a long illness. It's been...rather difficult. I thought perhaps the best thing would be to-to start fresh, to make a complete change, to...tackle a new adventure."

Ellery said automatically, "I'm sorry for your loss." *Did* this make a difference to his decision-making?

Mr. Peabody continued, "As Mr. Chandler said, 'One would think a writer would be happy here—if a writer is ever happy anywhere.'"

Ellery's ears pricked up. "Raymond Chandler?"

"Yes." Mr. Peabody beamed.

Ellery did not read Raymond Chandler any more than he read Mary Roberts Rinehart, but (thanks to Nora) he knew who Raymond Chandler was, so this was probably more knowledge of the genre than any of his previous job applicants had demonstrated.

Unsettling memories flashed through his mind like pictures in a flipbook.

Addison Something-or-other waving her report card in his face. The cat lady with the prison record. Disgruntled Dick Dix. The terrifying Ms. Puckett. The hipster chick-magnet. To name only a few—the few who'd looked most promising on paper.

Mr. Peabody interrupted his thoughts with another of those diffident coughs.

"Also, and again, I don't know that this would have any impact on your thinking, I'm not as concerned with salary as I am in finding a useful and interesting occupation."

"You're *not* concerned with salary?" Ellery couldn't help the note of wariness that crept into his voice.

"I appreciate cold hard cash as much as the next person," admitted Mr. Peabody, "but I have my retirement and a small, very small, income from my little hobby. My financial needs are not what they were when I had three daughters to put through college." He smiled reminiscently.

Ellery listened to the silence from the sales floor. It seemed to him to have an attentive quality rather than the usual appalled vibration. He decided then and there to make an executive decision.

He rose from behind the desk and offered his hand. "You're hired, Mr. Peabody. Come and meet the crew of the Crow's Nest."

"I know I've seen his face before," Nora was saying as Mr. Peabody's trim figure disappeared out of the corner windows and vanished from view.

Ellery was a little surprised at Nora's lack of enthusiasm over his decision to hire Mr. Peabody. He'd thought Mr. Peabody was exactly the kind of person Nora would approve of. The man could quote Raymond Chandler, for crying out loud.

But…not so much.

"He used to vacation on Buck Island with his wife. Maybe you recognize him from back then."

Nora shook her head. "I don't think so. I seem to recall seeing his likeness in black and white."

"You mean like a newspaper photo?"

"Perhaps." She sounded doubtful.

Ellery teased, "You mean like a mug shot?"

Nora brows drew together, but Ellery's cell phone rang—Jack was calling—and that was the end of the conversation.

"The ME's preliminary indicates accidental death." Jack was crisp and to the point.

"That can't be right."

"Sure it could. You've seen that staircase."

"Come on, Jack. That's too much of a coincidence. She has a fatal fall the very night she gets out of the hospital?"

"She didn't die last night. Death probably occurred between two and four o'clock yesterday afternoon. We won't know for sure until the autopsy is complete, but that's the way it looks to the ME as of now."

"You mean..."

"I mean it looks like she died not long after the taxi dropped her off."

It took Ellery a few moments to think of an answer. "Maybe he was waiting for her."

Jack said patiently, "Like I said, we don't have the autopsy report yet. It's not impossible that he was waiting for her, but he'd have to sneak past Officer Martin, who was parked outside the gates."

"You had Martin posted outside the house?"

"I did. At least till Miss Blackwell arrived home and ordered him off her property."

Ellery winced. Poor Miss Blackwell.

Jack said, "If your theory is correct and Miss Blackwell's prowler is this Robin Mann, gaining access to the house by using his old key..."

"How would he have gotten past Officer Martin? I see what you're getting at."

"It's too soon to draw any conclusions. But right now, coincidence or not, it *appears* that Miss Blackwell suffered a fatal accident."

"But all that stuff we found in the tunnel," Ellery protested. "The Rufus Blackwell costume. The stolen meat-loaf tin. The empty bourbon bottle. Sneaking into the Salty Dog. Why *would* Mann be hiding in the tunnels if not for some criminal reason? He, *someone*, attacked me in her home. He was... He was clearly up to no good!"

Jack let Ellery finish without interruption before saying mildly, "You realize you sound disappointed that Miss Blackwell wasn't murdered?"

"I'm not disappointed! I just don't believe it."

"And maybe you're right. Someone has definitely been up to no good. Does that mean they ultimately committed murder? We don't know yet. I can't assume anything. *You* can't assume anything."

Ellery sighed. "No, I know what you're saying. You're right. If the evidence isn't there, it isn't there."

"Not every criminal investigation ends with the case being solved."

"I know."

"Sometimes, even when you have the solution, you don't have enough evidence to make an arrest."

"I know."

Neither spoke for a moment.

"Okay. Well, I've got to go," Jack said. "I'll call you tomorrow, okay?"

That was Jack's way of letting Ellery know they would not be getting together that night. Which was a good thing, given that Ellery had gone ahead and made other plans.

"Yes. Talk to you then."

Jack disconnected.

Jack was right. Ellery knew he was right. But it still bothered him that someone cold enough, cruel enough to haunt a frightened old lady was probably going to get away with murder.

CHAPTER EIGHTEEN

"What do you do when you're not selling books or solving mysteries?" Robert asked.

They were having dinner at Wine and Rosés, a trendy little wine bar in Pirate's Cove. In fact, it was the *only* wine bar in Pirate's Cove. Along with a great wine list, proper crystal stemware, and terrific service, Wine and Rosés provided a really nice spread of cheeses, fruits, nuts, and meats. Ellery had almost forgotten what it was like to eat (and drink) at a place like this.

"I play Scrabble." He was kind of kidding, kind of not. Currently, he was the reigning champion of the Monday Night Scrabblers, although he'd missed the last two game nights while recovering from his concussion, so perhaps his crown was in peril.

Robert's eyes brightened. "Are you serious? I love Scrabble. It's probably my favorite game."

"If you like games, you should join the Monday Night Scrabblers."

"We have something called Monday Night Scrabblers?"

"We do, yeah. Invitation only. Mostly we play Scrabble, though some people prefer other games."

"Philistines." Over the rim of his wineglass, Robert's green eyes smiled into Ellery's.

It had been like this all evening—light and fun and flirty—and Ellery was having a good time. He liked Robert. Not as much as he liked Jack—that went without saying. Robert made no bones about being romantically interested in Ellery, and that was liable to prove a hindrance to friendship, but so far so good.

Robert had grown up in Ashland, Oregon, so he was very familiar with the Oregon Shakespeare Festival. He was both a theatergoer and film buff. He was apologetic about never having seen the *Happy Halloween! You're Dead!* movies.

"It shows you have a discerning palate," Ellery assured him.

"How is it you got involved in solving mysteries?" Robert cracked a pistachio nut with his long, strong fingers.

Ellery was about to reply when he was interrupted by a familiar voice.

"Well, well, stranger!" Dylan Carter, his girlfriend September in tow, stopped by their table.

"*Hey.* Long time no see," Ellery returned.

Dylan's lively blue eyes moved from Ellery to Robert and back again. He arched an eyebrow in inquiry.

Ellery gave an infinitesimal shake of his head.

Sure about that?

This was why Ellery had known it was paramount to talk to Jack before going out with Robert. The village hotline was no doubt already ablaze with news of their breakup.

He rolled his eyes. *I'm sure.*

Dylan grinned. He had been Team Jack from the beginning.

Ellery made the introductions, and Dylan and Robert chatted briefly. September looked vaguely bored, speaking when spoken to, but otherwise seeming to tune out the conversation around her.

"Have you solved our latest murder yet?" Dylan asked Ellery.

September sighed and offered Robert a smile of sympathy.

Ellery shook his head. "It sounds like Miss Blackwell's death really was an accident. Robert was telling me earlier that she had heart problems. But she didn't want to hear about it. She checked herself out of the hospital early, against his advice."

Robert looked pained, so maybe that wasn't supposed to be public knowledge.

Dylan said, "Really? Well, I guess that's easier to believe than that we have *another* murderer running around Pirate's Cove."

"True," Ellery admitted.

"By the way, I don't know what you said to Sue when you had your run-in, but she hasn't dared print a word about you since."

"She didn't seem all that cowed when I ran into her Wednesday."

"No? Well, I had no idea you were involved in this even peripherally. In fact, I don't think she ran more than an obituary on Miss Blackwell today. A pretty uninspired one at that."

Robert asked what the beef was between Ellery and Sue, and Dylan filled him in with a slightly exaggerated version of the war between Ellery and the editor of the *Scuttlebutt Weekly*.

By then, the waitress had brought their bill, which Robert insisted on grabbing. He slapped down one of those platinum American Express cards heavy enough to double as a door stop, and then signed his name with the usual indecipherable physician's scrawl.

Studying that black slash of signature, Ellery couldn't help thinking the last name looked more like Mann than Mane.

It brought him up short. Just for an instant.

Plenty of people had the initials RM.

Robert was too young to be Robin.

And too old to be Robin's son.

He could be Robin's brother?

Okay, which was it? He was Robin or Robin's son or Robin's brother? All of this based on having the same initials?

Jack would say that Ellery was starting to see mysteries where none existed. And Jack would be right.

Still. It was quite a coincidence, right?

He and Robert left the restaurant with Dylan and the now openly yawning September, who murmured a protesting, "*Dilly*," when Dylan asked Ellery how his new play was coming along. In addition to owning the Toy Chest, the shop next door to the Crow's Nest, Dylan ran the Scallywags, Pirate's Cove's local amateur theater guild.

"It's not," Ellery admitted.

"It will," Dylan assured him. "You'll see. You're just feeling the pressure of having a hit right out of the gate."

"Uh, sure. That's what it is."

Even September laughed at that.

They said their good-nights, and Ellery and Robert climbed into Robert's black Infiniti Q60.

"You're also working on a play?" Robert asked.

Ellery groaned.

Robert laughed. "Was that *yes, no*, or *I think it's appendicitis*?"

"More like *don't remind me*."

Within a couple of minutes Robert drew up in front of the Crow's Nest.

As Ellery gazed through the brightly lit windows, he felt a flicker of unease. Though it was ten thirty, every light in the bookshop seemed to be on, despite the fact that he'd turned them off when he'd locked up earlier.

"I had a great time tonight, Ellery." Robert's voice recalled him to the present. "I'd like to see you again."

"I had a great time too," Ellery replied, which was true.

"Can I call you?"

"Sure. I'd like that. I'd like to be friends."

Robert considered, acknowledged the message with a small smile. "Sounds good to me. I'll give you a call soon. Have you toured North Point lighthouse yet?"

"Not yet. Sounds like fun." Ellery got out of the car, feeling in his pocket for his keys. On impulse, he bent down and said, "Hey, by any chance are you related to Robin Mann?"

That was the wine talking. Ordinarily, he would have tried to be a little more tactful, a little more cautious. But they'd had *a lot* of wine and not much food.

"Who?" In the greenish glow of the dome light, Robert looked totally blank.

"Robin Mann."

"No. Who's Robin Mann?"

"It doesn't matter."

Robert's face changed. His eyes widened, his mouth opened, and he burst out laughing. "Oh my God. Am I part of your case? Am I a *suspect*?"

"No, of course not," Ellery said quickly, hoping his face wasn't as red as it felt. "I just wondered—"

"I *am*. I'm a suspect. Is that why you went out with me?"

Ellery said quickly, "*No*. No, I really did have a great time."

"Oh my God, how funny is that?"

Pretty funny, apparently, since Robert was still chortling loudly as he drove away.

That was embarrassing.

He was going to have to trade in his deerstalker for a dunce cap.

But after all, every theory couldn't be right.

And it wasn't like Ellery had actually formed any *theory* about Dr. Robert Mane. He'd happened to notice the similarity of Mane's name to his actual suspect's name. That was all. Assuming Robin Mann even had anything to do with anything happening in Pirate's Cove.

Wendy Parrish had yet to return his phone message. Maybe that was suspicious?

Probably not.

But you never knew. Most homicides were committed by family members. Granted, that included spouses and ex-spouses and probably ex-boyfriends.

The good news was Mane had seemed amused and not offended.

The other good news was Jack would never hear about this. He sure as heck would never hear about it from Ellery.

Ellery let himself into the Crow's Nest. He sniffed the air. Someone had brewed a fresh pot of coffee not too long ago.

"Nora?"

No answer.

"Hello? Anybody here?"

Silence.

Weird.

He had definitely turned the lights off before he left that evening to drop Watson off at his puppysitter.

Well, maybe Nora had come back for something.

But no, she wouldn't forget to turn off the lights. He groaned softly. He was tired after exploring the tunnels with Jack the night before. He had drunk too much wine. He just wanted to grab Watson, and head home to his own comfortable bed.

But as he walked through the brightly lit shop, he noticed that, in addition to all the lights being on, chairs had been set up in a horseshoe as if for a meeting of the Silver Sleuths.

He stopped in his tracks.

"I'm calling an emergency meeting of the Silver Sleuths tonight," Nora had said.

It looked like a meeting had indeed been called, so where were the Silver Sleuths?

The coffee maker had been turned off, but the pot was still warm, so they had only recently called it a night.

Called it a night but forgot to turn off the lights?

A folded paper lay beneath one of the chairs. Ellery retrieved the square, unfolded it, and studied the rudimentary drawing.

A map.

As he realized what he was looking at, he felt his hair stand on end.

You. Are. Here.

And the Silver Sleuths?

By now? They were at the Black House.

* * * * *

"No. They wouldn't. Why would they? They wouldn't."

And yet, somehow Ellery was sure they had.

"But why? Why now? Why this case?" Ellery punctuated these unknowables with periodic slaps on the steering wheel.

Was it because they felt a personal connection to this case? Did they feel some responsibility for Miss Blackwell's demise? Did they feel Jack and PICO PD had dropped the ball?

Or, most alarming of all, had the Silver Sleuths tired of watching from the sidelines? Did they now wish to play a bigger role in what they frequently referred to as *their* investigations?

"Think of what you've unleashed upon this unsuspecting island," he told himself.

The VW bounced and banged over the dirt road winding through the hills as Ellery sped toward the Black House. He tried to reassure himself there was no danger. There was a very good chance they wouldn't be able to even get inside.

The police tape would surely discourage even Nora from—

Who was he kidding? Nora had probably picked the front-door lock by now, and the Silver Sleuths were in position, lying in wait for the murderer to show up.

Except there was no murderer.

According to Jack *and* Robert Mane, Miss Blackwell had probably died of an accidental fall. It happened all the time. Falls were the second leading cause of unintentional injury deaths worldwide. How about that for a comforting statistic. The fact that someone had been trying for days, maybe weeks to bring about that very result didn't mean Miss Blackwell hadn't managed it all on her own.

Robin Mann or whoever was trying to bring about Miss Blackwell's early demise (assuming that had been the goal of dressing up like a ghost and skulking around her home) had no reason to return to the Blackwell estate now.

Did he?

If the goal had been to kill Miss Blackwell, mission accomplished.

If the goal had been to find something—a copy of a deed, a will, a birth certificate—surely, he'd found it by now?

If the goal had been to *plant* something—a deed, a will, a birth certificate—surely, Mann had done that by now?

Maybe not.

The fact that the prowler kept returning to the Black House might indicate he hadn't succeeded in whatever his plan was. Opportunities to do so had been limited after Miss Blackwell's accident. Especially since the guy couldn't stop snacking long enough to focus on the job at hand. Having been surprised by Ellery mid fridge raid, the Hamburglar might not have had another chance to carry out his mission. Jack had posted Officer Martin at the house right after that.

Okay, but Ellery knew from firsthand experience how easy it was to scale the stone wall surrounding the property. And, no disrespect to Officer Martin, he wasn't the most experienced member of PICO PD. It wasn't impossible someone could slip past him. It wasn't impossible he had simply sat in his car the whole time and never bothered to check the house doors or windows. Still, most potential evil-doers were going to find the sight of a police presence, however slight, discouraging.

About half a mile from the Blackwell estate, Ellery pulled off the road and parked beneath some straggly scrub oaks. He got out, locked the door, and looked around. There were no lights coming from the hillside vacation homes, and not many in the village below.

Maybe he had this wrong.

Would the Silver Sleuths really carry through with...what the heck *were* they planning? To capture the prowler themselves? God. Surely not. But he could practically hear Nora now trying to make a citizen's arrest.

For all they knew, this guy was armed.

No. As much as Ellery wanted to rely on Nora's sense of self-preservation, he wasn't sure she had one.

He started up the road, sticking to the shadows, half walking, half jogging. It was a lot longer walk than drive, for sure. The night felt cool against his flushed face. He drew in measured lungsful of air that still smelled of wildflowers.

Once, when he paused for breath, he thought he saw a flash of light on the hillside above him. Headlights maybe? He didn't see it again.

All the same, as Ellery raced up the road, trying to pace himself and doing his best not to trip over the dips and runnels in the road, he kept having the uncomfortable feeling he was being watched.

Maybe that was his guilty conscience. Jack would *not* approve of any of this.

But hopefully Jack would never learn of this misstep by the Silver Sleuths.

Out of breath and damp with sweat, Ellery at last reached the tall gates of the Blackwell estate. He slipped inside.

Still keeping to the shadows as much as possible, he ran up the drive. There were no cars, no indication anyone was on the property. Given recent events, that didn't mean much, but if the Silver Sleuths had been faced with hiking up that road, their plan could well have ended then and there.

Ellery reached the front porch. He'd been expecting to see crime-scene tape across the door, but there was none. Did that mean Miss Blackwell's death had officially been determined to be accidental?

He cupped his face with his hands, peering through one of the windows. He could make out nothing but shadowy shapes.

Nothing moved.

There was not a sound.

It was *so* quiet, he began to have doubts. He couldn't picture the Silver Sleuths staying silent for more than a minute. Maybe he'd wronged them, and even now they were tucked in their beds like responsible senior citizens dreaming whatever responsible senior citizens dreamed of.

However. Now that he was here, maybe he should just take a peek inside...

Damn.

He no longer had a key. He'd returned Miss Blackwell's key to her when he'd dropped off her books at the med center. He'd have to try to gain entrance through the side door with the sticky lock.

Unless...

On impulse, Ellery grasped the front-door handle, and the door opened a crack.

His hopes sank.

No way had Jack left a possible crime scene unsecured. If Ellery had needed proof that Nora was on the premises, this was it.

He stepped inside the close, musty interior and pushed the door shut behind him.

It took his eyes a moment to adjust. The starlight had been bright compared to the front hall of the Black House. He could barely see the staircase, despite pallid light filtering through the stained-glass window, but he was pretty sure someone was crouched on the landing.

"Nora?" he hissed. "I know you're in here."

The darkness seemed to flutter into life, *shushing* sounds coming from different parts of the long room.

"What's *he* doing here?" Miss Smith's voice protested.

"He's going to spoil everything!" Mr. Starling exclaimed.

Ellery began, "You guys, you can't—this is tres—"

SHHHHHHHH!!!

"Don't *shush* me. Do you know how much trouble you'll be in if Jack ever finds out about this?"

Funny thing, just for a second, he thought he smelled Jack's aftershave.

"Really, Ellery, your timing couldn't be worse," Mrs. Nelson said in normal tones.

She too was promptly *shushed.*

"*My* timing?" Irritatingly, he seemed to be talking to a hat rack. Where the heck were they all hiding? The room felt crowded with people but he couldn't see anyone. It was like arguing with ventriloquists.

From down the hall, Mrs. Ferris whispered frantically, "He's coming! He's coming! I see him. I see him. Bogey at high noon!"

A slight shadow scurried out of the hall, passed him, and vanished behind the heavy velvet drapes.

Bogey at what the what?

The grandfather clock Ellery stood beside muttered, "Not *now*, dearie." A bony hand closed around Ellery's wrist and yanked him back into the corner. Even in the murky light, he could see the excitement gleaming in Nora's eyes.

Holy hell. It was going down.

Whatever *it* was.

His heart was thumping so loudly, he almost missed the creak of a floorboard. A tall silhouette appeared in the doorway at the far end of the room. The figure paused.

No body moved. Ellery wasn't sure anyone so much as breathed.

Did the intruder sense a trap? Was he trying to get his bearings?

Ellery's heart skipped a beat, possibly two. Nora sucked in a sharp breath.

"*Surprise!*" screamed Miss Smith.

Nora pushed past Ellery. Six dazzling beams of light focused like lasers on the astonished man—burglar?—frozen in the doorway. Mouth agape, he blinked in the glare of flashlight and cell-phone beams.

"Take the shot, take the shot!" Nora cried.

Wait. What?

Mr. Starling stepped out of cover and snapped a photo with his cell phone. Actually, he snapped several photos; it sounded like the paparazzi were on scene.

"Ha! Got you!" Mr. Starling declared.

That snapped the intruder out of his trance. He made a swipe at Mr. Starling's phone, sending the phone and Stanley flying.

"*Oof,*" Mr. Starling said. Or words to that effect.

"Get him! Get him!" Nora shrieked.

That seemed to be Ellery's job, unless he wanted to stand there and watch the Silver Sleuths get obliterated. He snapped back to life and tackled the intruder around his waist. They went flying backward, landing on the hardwood floor with a house-shaking *thud.*

Been there done that.

Only this time, Ellery had the advantage of surprise. At least until, alarmingly, the Silver Sleuths tried to provide backup. Even so, he managed to deliver a couple of solid punches despite the small fist pounding repeatedly and distractingly on his back as though urgently seeking directions.

"What the hell?" yelled the intruder, and then, "*Owww!*" as someone clunked him over the head with what was probably a flashlight, given that flashlight beams were swinging wildly against the walls and ceiling like searchlights amidst an air raid.

Suddenly, it was over.

"*Police! Put down your weapons!*"

Even mid-brawl, Ellery recognized that voice and groaned inwardly.

A forest of police boots and uniformed limbs appeared in the bouncing spotlights. Hard hands yanked him to his feet and shoved him aside. The room lights came on, blinding everyone for an instant. Men in blue hauled the intruder upright, felt him down for weapons—which he did not have—and snapped handcuffs on him.

The intruder shook his head as though half stunned and glared at his captors. "What do you think you're doing? I own this property! I have every right to be here."

"Is that so?" Jack's smile was sardonic.

Was this the same guy he'd found scarfing down jam and cottage cheese? Ellery wasn't sure for a moment. For one thing, this intruder was neatly dressed in business casual trousers and sportscoat. He was clean shaved. His hair and eyebrows were jet-black. Frankly, he *did* look like someone who had every right to be there.

"Yes, it's so. My name is Robin Mann. If you'll allow me to reach into my coat pocket, I can show you identification and my copy of Miss Blackwell's will."

"Good heavens." Nora peered at the man in custody. "I think it *is* him."

Jack turned to Ellery. "Is this the guy who attacked you and threw you in the cellar?"

As Robin Mann's blue gaze met Ellery's, his eyes hardened with animosity.

Oh yeah. It was the same guy all right. Ellery recognized that look. The hair was different and Mann might smell different, but all the showers in the world couldn't wash away the cold calculation behind those eyes.

He nodded. "That's him."

"Book him," Jack said to his officers.

"On what charge?" Mann protested. "I tell you, I'm Juliet's rightful heir!"

"We'll start with assault and battery, and go from there." Jack jerked his head toward the door, and the officers hustled Mann, still protesting loudly, outside. The door slammed shut behind them.

Jack turned back to the remaining participants of the evening's festivities.

"What is the *matter* with you people?" he shouted.

The question was rhetorical because, as the Silver Sleuths all began to speak at once, Jack cut in with a loud, "I don't want to hear it! Do you kooks not realize what could have happened tonight?"

Again, the Silver Sleuths all started talking at the same time.

"There was really no danger." Nora tried to soothe him. "We weren't going to take any unnecessary chances."

"Not take unnecessary chances?" Ellery spluttered.

"What happened tonight is we caught a villain in the act," Mrs. Clarence informed Jack. "We have evidence right here. Right there. Show him your phone, Stanley."

Mr. Starling, hobbling to retrieve his phone, held it up in triumph, then swore. "My screen is cracked!"

Understatement of the year.

"Were you here the whole time?" Mrs. Ferris demanded of Jack. She seemed ever so slightly put-out.

Jack closed his eyes as though summoning superhuman strength. "Yes, Mrs. Ferris, PICO PD was conducting surveillance this evening with the intention of apprehending a suspect while in commission of a crime. Which you— You people almost blew."

"Oh, that was so clever of you!" Nora said admiringly. "Never once did I realize anyone else was here." She turned to Mrs. Nelson. "Did you realize, Hermione?"

"They were quiet as mice," Mrs. Nelson agreed.

"Do you not realize he could have had a weapon?" Jack exclaimed. "Someone could have been seriously injured."

"No, no. Ellery had him under control," Nora assured him.

Ellery threw Jack an alarmed look and shook his head.

"So the case is solved," Mrs. Smith said slowly, wonderingly. "We actually did it! We solved a case."

The other Silver Sleuths shared delighted—and equally surprised—looks. They proceeded to high five each other.

Jack made a strangled sound. "That's it," he said. "You're *all* under arrest."

CHAPTER NINETEEN

It was very possible they *were* all under arrest.

However, there was not enough room in the Pirate's Cove jail to hold all the evening's detainees, so at sunrise, Ellery and the Silver Sleuths were still sitting in the police station reception area.

Aside from offers of medical assistance and permission to use the restrooms—the latter of which, the Silver Sleuths had repeatedly taken advantage of—they had been left strictly alone. Far from being chastened, Nora and her Over-the-Hill Gang seemed to be basking in the glow of victory.

Ellery? Not so much.

"You know, Jack's right. Somebody could easily have been badly hurt tonight," he'd tried to tell Nora earlier.

She'd only patted his hand in an absent *there, there* sort of way.

The others *pshawed* the very notion.

"If Chief Carson didn't want us there, he shouldn't have let us inside," Mrs. Smith said.

It wasn't the first time she'd tried to float that idea. Jack had shot it down the first time, and Ellery shot it down now.

"You know why he let you enter. For the same reason he let me enter. It was too late to stop any of us without alerting Mann. Just be glad nobody got hurt and we didn't mess up Jack's operation."

He might as well have saved his breath. They all seemed to think PICO PD's on scene presence was mere coincidence, and *they* had apprehended Robin Mann. When Mr. Starling began to boast about how useful his long-ago jujitsu training had come in, Ellery half hoped Jack *would* lock them up for a few days.

"Did you really think Mann was going to stand there and let you place him under citizen's arrest?"

Nora looked surprised. "We weren't going to try to arrest him. We were simply after photographic proof that he was in the house and had the opportunity to salt the mine."

"To what?"

"To plant a fake will that would prove he was Juliet's legal heir."

"But Nora, how would taking his photo prove anything unless you actually caught him, mid-act, placing the will in a flower pot or something? And even then. Plus, he could claim the photo was doctored."

"No. We're all witnesses to his attempt to plant the fake will."

"But—but then my question remains the same. Did you really think he'd stand there and let you snap his photo?"

Nora sighed, admitted, "I did think we'd be able to make a faster getaway."

She seemed to conveniently forget her shrieked orders to *Get him! Get him!*

Ellery groaned. "Why wouldn't you tell *me* what you were planning?"

Nora looked apologetic. "You'd have tried to stop us, dearie. You'd have felt obligated to tell Chief Carson."

"I sure as heck would've!"

Nora's shrug seemed to say, *There you have it!* "Now that you're dating Chief Carson, we don't want to put you in an awkward position." She added honestly, "Unless there's no other way."

"Mann could have been *armed*, Nora. He could have shot someone. He could have shot *you*. Did any of you consider that?"

"No, no." She corrected hastily, "That is, *yes*, we considered it. We discussed the possibility. It seemed most unlikely given that his plan was to try to claim the estate through legal channels. How would he explain shooting one of us? Let alone all of us. That wouldn't have fit in with his scheme at all."

"There are so many assumptions there, I don't know where to begin. He was willing to kill Miss Blackwell. He probably *did* kill her."

"But that was different. Anyway, the ME be-
lieves her injuries indicate an accident." Her tone
grew reflective. "Had we known what Chief Carson
was up to, perhaps we wouldn't have felt the situation
was so dire. I had no idea you'd told him so much. Or
that he actually paid attention."

Ellery gave a disbelieving laugh. "You make it
sound like this was Jack's fault for not keeping you
informed about *his* investigation."

Nora chuckled. "That would hardly be fair."

And *that* was hardly convincing.

The hours ticked by.

Outside the tinted windows of the police station,
the sun rose high in the cloudless blue sky. It was going to be a beautiful day.

Some of the defiance drained out of the Silver
Sleuths. They did not like missing the breakfast spe-
cials at the Blue Galleon. They were getting stiff and
tired after hours of waiting in the uncomfortable reception area chairs. Mr. Starling's wife had already
phoned to report him missing. Mrs. Nelson and Mrs.
Clarence speculated uneasily as to what their hus-
bands would say if they were slapped with fines.

Ellery knew from terse behind-the-front-desk
conversations that Robin Mann was still in interrogation, but how that interrogation was going, remained
an open question.

When ten thirty rolled around, they were *still* sitting in the reception area, and the Silver Sleuths' spirits were running lower than their Geritol. Nora uncomfortably apologized for the fact that the Crow's Nest was not open for business, and the others soberly joined in the commiserations.

Ellery had started to doze off when his cell phone rang. He jerked his head up, peered blearily at the screen. He didn't recognize the number but saw it was located in Newport.

"Can I step outside to answer this?" he asked Mac, the desk sergeant.

The sergeant glanced at Jack's closed door, growled, "Make it fast," and returned to his paperwork.

"Ellery Page speaking." Ellery pushed out through the front doors, blinking at the bright sunlight. A gull, perched atop the flag pole, *ha-ha-ha-ha*-ed at him.

"Mr. Page? This is Wendy Parrish." Mrs. Parrish had a brisk, pleasant voice. "Sorry it took so long to get back to you. I've been visiting my daughter in Minnesota."

"Mrs. Parrish, thanks for returning my phone call." His stomach knotted as he realized she probably didn't know her aunt had died.

She gave a funny laugh. "I admit I was a little surprised to hear from you. My great-aunt has never shown the least interest in connecting with her family. I gave up trying years ago."

"I'm sorry," Ellery said—and then her words registered. "Did you say Miss Blackwell was your *great*-aunt?"

"That's right." She sounded amused as she added, "I've never actually met her. She's always kept to herself."

Ellery said slowly, "So you're not Cressida's daughter?"

"Cressida? No." Mrs. Parrish laughed. "I never met Great-aunt Cressida either. In fact, I never met any of them. The Buck Island Blackwells. From what I understand, that branch of the family was always a little...odd."

This was strange, right?

He waited for her to stop speaking. "Would you know how to get in contact with Cressida?"

"Me? No."

"Do you think there's anyone on your side of the family who might know where she went after she married?"

"No. *Did* she marry?" Mrs. Parrish sounded doubtful. "I always thought she must have died young."

She continued speaking, but Ellery, stricken by a sudden and shocking suspicion, didn't hear a word she said.

He really hadn't seen this coming. This changed *everything*.

When she came to another pause, he asked, "I'm sorry, but why do you think she died young?"

"Who?"

"Your—Cressida."

Something in his tone must have alerted her. Mrs. Parrish said cautiously, "It's only that genealogy is a hobby of mine. Well, honestly, it's sort of my passion. Cressida dropped out of our family history forty-three years ago. I've never been able to find any trace of her anywhere. No marriage certificate, no driver's license, no passport application...no nothing."

"I...see."

He did. Finally.

She added cheerfully, "I've never found any proof that she died either, so what does that tell you?"

What indeed?

* * * * *

When Ellery stepped back inside the reception area, the desk sergeant said ominously, "He wants to see you next."

No question who *he* was. The Silver Sleuths cast him commiserating looks of farewell as Ellery headed to Jack's office.

"Come," Jack called crisply in answer to Ellery's knock.

Ellery opened the door.

From behind the desk, Jack gave him a long, long look.

"I went there to stop them," Ellery protested. "You were there—somewhere—you had to have heard."

"I heard and saw enough to know there's a fifty-fifty chance you'd have gone inside either way."

Ellery sighed. "Maybe. Since I was already there. But it wasn't premeditated."

Jack shook his head as though it was hopeless. He pointed his pen at the chair in front of his desk, and Ellery sat down.

"Mann admits everything," Jack told him.

"That's great!"

"Except murder."

"What? But that's ridiculous. Of course he killed her."

"He swears up and down that the first he knew Miss Blackwell was dead was when he saw her obituary in the *Scuttlebutt Weekly*."

Ellery frowned. "He's got to be lying, right?"

"I'm not sure," Jack admitted.

Ellery did a doubletake. "You're not?"

"No. I'm not." He proceeded to bring Ellery up to speed on his investigation into Robin Mann's background.

After his relationship with Juliet Blackwell had ended, Mann returned to the mainland and, shortly after, became the permanent escort of a widowed society matron by the name of Peggy London. When that relationship had ended, Mann had wooed and won Genieve Finley, a socially awkward rich girl who loved horses, hunting and the Hamptons. Genieve had been followed by Martha Mott, a very elderly and very eccentric patron of the arts with a very protective family.

When Martha had passed on to that great art gallery in the sky, Mann had found himself out in the cold, financially speaking, and getting a little long in the tooth for the professional escort biz.

"How did you find all this out so fast?" Ellery asked. "I was still trying to figure out which Robin Mann was the right one.

Jack gave him a look of disbelief. "I'm in law enforcement. I have resources you don't. That's why I can do this for a living. I have the training and the tools."

"Er, right. Of course," Ellery said hastily. "Were you able to find out if any of Mann's lady friends died under suspicious circumstances?"

"Nope. Not a one. That's not to say he's a choirboy. He stole from them, he lied, he cheated, he manipulated. He's most definitely a bad guy. But until now, he's been a nonviolent bad guy."

"But he obviously planned on murdering Miss Blackwell. How else does he explain lurking around her house dressed like Rufus Blackwell."

"That's the thing," Jack said. "He doesn't deny faking her will. He doesn't deny trying to, in his words, *hurry her along*, but he claims he had nothing to do with her death. He says he didn't return to the house until last night."

"That's impossible."

"It's not impossible. I admit, I'm having trouble believing it, but the ME is going to rule accidental death."

"You're kidding."

"No. And here's the thing. The afternoon Miss Blackwell died, Mann had already checked into the Seacrest Inn. He has an alibi."

Ellery's mouth dropped. "He..."

"Yep."

They were each silent with their thoughts. "Maybe it *was* an accident," Ellery said finally, doubtfully. "I mean, if the ME still thinks so..."

"Yep. According to the ME, all indications are Miss Blackwell lost her balance and tumbled down the staircase. She had a weak heart as it turns out."

"Yes, that's what Robert said."

Jack's brows shot up. "Robert?"

"Dr. Mane."

Jack's brows flattened into a straight, dark line. "I see."

Ellery changed the subject. "So it *could* have happened that way. But why was Mann hiding out in the tunnels?"

Jack grimaced. "He was afraid that if he was staying locally, the timing would look suspicious once he showed up as Miss Blackwell's rightful heir."

"That *would* be one heck of a coincidence."

"He remembered the tunnels from when he lived on the island, and decided that camping underground was the perfect solution. He wasn't far wrong. He was able to move around the village without ever being seen buying so much as a coffee."

"The Invisible Mann." Ellery chewed this new information over. "But why did he leave the tunnels before Miss Blackwell was dead?"

"After he tangled with you at the Black House, he felt his situation was becoming precarious. He decided to go a different route."

"What route?"

Jack shook his head. "He assures me improvisation is one of his strengths."

"I don't doubt it. So he admits planning to replace Miss Blackwell's will with a fake will leaving everything to himself."

"Yes."

"And he admits trying to scare her to death."

"Yes."

"But he denies actually killing her."

"That's the gist of it."

Ellery said tentatively, "And you believe him?"

Jack said, "I don't disbelieve him."

"Really?"

"Really."

Ellery asked curiously, "Who *did* Miss Blackwell leave everything to?"

"No one. According to her lawyer, she died in-testate. But at one time, Mann was listed as her sole beneficiary. He was betting that hadn't changed—which was seriously overestimating both his charms and Miss Blackwell's unforgivingness. He was all prepared with a new will, in case she *had* changed the old."

"He'd forged a new will?"

"Not exactly. He'd made a copy of the original will back when they were still living together. Just in case."

"In case of *what*?"

"We're never going to get the full story out of him. My take? This was on his back burner for years. Not necessarily committing murder. I think that came about out of desperation. He didn't figure on her liv-ing so long. In fact, he expressed irritation at her lon-gevity. But he definitely intended to show up at the right time and the right place with a duly witnessed will naming himself her sole heir. He admits he al-ways considered her his retirement plan."

"He's been planning this for *twenty years*?"

"Again, I think this was one of many irons in many fires. As he began to run out of options, Miss Blackwell and her millions of dollars' worth of real estate began to look more and more enticing."

Ellery shook his head. "He almost got away it."

Jack said with grim satisfaction, "Yep. If he hadn't strolled right into the trap we set."

"Along with the rest of us."

"Yes."

"Which, in fairness, nobody knew about."

Jack said gravely, "My apologies. But being the police chief, I occasionally, *just* to keep my hand in, like to involve myself in some of our high-profile cases. I hope that's acceptable?"

Ellery made a face. "Okay, you don't have to be sarcastic."

Jack snorted. "Don't I? It's better than the alternative."

Jack had been pretty irate the night before, so yeah, a little sarcasm was only to be expected. In fact, the *least* to be expected.

"Again, for the record, I went there to stop them," Ellery said.

"I know. I heard." Jack rubbed his temples.

"It's like trying to stop a train."

Jack's sigh was longer than said train whistle. "I know. Believe me. I know."

Ellery considered what he'd learned on the phone a little while earlier. "I have a theory."

"Let's hear it." Jack sounded more resigned than interested.

"I think Miss Blackwell recognized Robin Mann. She suspected what he was up to. I think she thought she'd outsmart him at his own game."

"Outsmart him how?"

"Arrange a fatal accident? Or maybe he'd just... disappear."

Jack's eyes narrowed. "That's quite an accusation."

"She did it before. Made someone disappear."

"What are you talking about?"

Ellery explained what he'd learned from Miss Blackwell's great-niece, finishing, "If I'm right, she got away with murder once—well, twice—before."

Jack said skeptically, "You think Miss Blackwell murdered her sister and her former fiancé and buried them in the cellar?"

"I do. I think that's why Miss Blackwell was so terrified of reporting what was happening to the police. She couldn't risk police snooping around and starting to ask questions."

"Yeah, but it's a real jump from not wanting to involve the police, to committing murder. How would she have pulled it off?"

"I think it would have been easier than you'd think. Most of the servants were gone by then. Edgar Blackwell was bedridden. Who was going to dare question her? Obviously, I don't have all the answers, but Miss Blackwell was smart, strong and determined."

"She'd also have to be crazy. Crazy enough to kill two people." But Jack sounded thoughtful.

"Maybe she was."

"What would be her motive?"

"Jealousy? Rage? Desperation? People do commit murder for those reasons. And for even crazier reasons."

Jack was frowning. "Sure. But even if Miss Blackwell could have pulled off the logistics of a double homicide, how could it go undetected for so many years?"

"Almost fifty years ago? I think it would've been pretty easy to hide Cressida's disappearance. Miss Blackwell could just tell people that Cressida had run off and she didn't want to talk about it. As for the fiancé, I'm not sure. Miss Blackwell could still claim plausible deniability. And, according to Nora, László Jeles was an immigrant *and* estranged from his family, so maybe nobody looked that hard once he disappeared? People here might easily assume the happy couple went back to Hungary. Even if somebody did look for him, would anyone really suspect Miss Blackwell?"

Jack opened his mouth. Ellery said, "Would your predecessor, the former police chief, have suspected Miss Blackwell?"

Jack's expression was pained. "No."

"I really do think that's why Miss Blackwell was so freaked out about anyone going into that cellar. For the record, that cellar is hella creepy. If there's any place in that house that's haunted, that's the spot. There's a large section of wall that's too big for a doorway, but just about right for a tomb. To me, it looks like it was bricked up by someone who didn't know what they were doing."

"It's hard to believe that in nearly half a century no one thought to ask Miss Blackwell where these two people might be."

"Maybe they did ask. Maybe she said she didn't know." Ellery shrugged.

Jack scowled, thinking.

"There's a for sure way to find out if I'm right," Ellery said.

Jack stared at him for a long moment. He reached for the phone.

* * * * *

A short time later, Ellery was walking out of the police station—to the dismay of the Silver Sleuths—just as Sue Lewis was walking in.

For an instant, he didn't recognize her. Sue looked years older, almost gray with weariness. Her normally coiffed hair was disheveled. She appeared to have slept in her clothes.

Their gazes met, and Sue seemed to recoil. She glanced past Ellery to where the Silver Sleuths continued to mill in the reception area, voicing their protests at "police brutality" (Jack had already warned Ellery he planned on holding them for the entire day) and she backed up.

Retreated.

It was such an odd, un-Sue-like reaction that it caught Ellery off-guard.

"Sue?"

He was speaking to her back. She was already striding toward the parking lot.

What the…

Since when?

He didn't for one second believe anything he'd said to Sue in any of their recent encounters would have sunk in, let alone cowed her, but there she was. All but running from him.

Running from *something*.

Just like that, the last little Scrabble tile fell into place. REVELATION.

Thirteen points.

"Sue, wait." Ellery sped after her.

Sue turned to face him, her stance like that of something at bay. "What do you want?" Her eyes were fierce, but they glittered with what he thought might be tears.

"I-I know what happened. I know it was an accident."

She went so pale, he was afraid she was going to faint.

"What are you *talking* about?" She turned away again, but she didn't take another step. "Leave me alone." Her voice was muffled.

"You went to interview Miss Blackwell after she was released from the hospital. Either she refused to speak to you or she wouldn't answer the door. But this time you weren't going to take no for an answer. Either she left the front unlocked or you went around to the side and found you could get in that way. You entered the house and you startled her coming down the grand staircase. She fell."

Sue whirled to face him. Her chest rose and fell as though she'd just finished a marathon. "You're so wrong," she panted. "You're so crazy."

"The ME says it was an accident. You never intended to harm her. You just wanted your story."

"What story? What do you know about it? You're..." She trailed off as though she'd literally run out of words.

Ellery said, "You figured it out too. Sooner than I did. You figured out that Miss Blackwell murdered her sister and former fiancé when they tried to run off together. You knew they had to be buried somewhere in the—"

He broke off at the raucous laughter that tore out of Sue's throat. Sue laughed and laughed and then started to cry.

"Oh my God. Wrong *again*. Once again, you've got it totally wrong. You're *so* stupid. Why does everyone think you're—You're an idiot savant—only without the savant part. I thought she'd murdered *him*. Robin Mann. That story about his disappearing in the night without a word to anyone. I was sure she'd killed him. You can't find anything about him on the internet. He scrubbed his internet presence. And she was obviously, *obviously* hiding something in that mausoleum. She fired the last of the servants. She wouldn't let anyone inside. She wouldn't let anyone speak his name." Sue hiccupped on a sob and then started that scary laughter again. "And all the time, he was planning to kill *her*."

Sue had her sources and had clearly heard about Mann's arrest and quickly put two and two together. Which meant, she had come to the police station to report her part in Miss Blackwell's death.

Which took guts. She didn't have to confess to anything. She wasn't under suspicion. The ME was about to rule Miss Blackwell's death an accident.

Ellery did not like Sue. He was never going to like Sue. So he was astonished to hear himself say, "Do you want me to go with you? To talk to Jack?"

Her eyes blazed. "Go with me to see *Jack*? No. I don't. I don't need or want *your* help, Ellery. I can talk to Jack on my own, thanks!"

She brushed past him, strode down the walkway, and vanished into the station.

EPILOGUE

GRAVE, SOLUTION, COMMITMENT, UNFOR-GIVING, BITTERSWEET...

Better late than never, Scrabble gods.

It was Sunday evening, one day after Sue Lewis had confessed to involuntary manslaughter and been released on her own recognizance. One day after Robin Mann had been charged with everything Jack could come up with.

Everything but homicide.

Squeak. Squeak. Squeak.

Ellery's game of Scrabble GO was interrupted by Watson, who dropped a slimy green rubber frog on his foot.

"Uh, thanks," Ellery said. "Does Jack know you nabbed his froggy?"

Watson grinned, waiting until Ellery picked up the squeak toy and threw it into the grass beyond the terrace. Watson bounded away, snatched up the frog, and gave it a good shake for putting him to all that trouble.

Ellery smiled faintly, returned to his game, but raised his head at the sound of tires on gravel.

What did it mean when you recognized the particular purr of a particular engine?

What did it mean that the particular engine you recognized was a cop car?

He set his phone on the pink marble table set for two, went down the steps, and walked around the side of the house. Jack was just climbing out of his SUV. He still wore his uniform, so he hadn't stopped by his cottage to change. Which probably meant he wasn't staying long.

Ellery sighed inwardly, but that was the reality of dating a cop. And when the cop was the chief of police? Multiply by ten. Jack was here now. That was the important thing.

"Hey," Jack said, and then "*Hey*," as Ellery walked straight into his arms.

Jack still looked very tired, and needed a shave, but he was smiling when the kiss ended. "What's that for?"

"Long time no see," Ellery said.

Not really, of course. Just a little over twenty-four hours since he'd seen or spoken to Jack. But somehow it felt like weeks.

"But always worth waiting for." Jack's eyes looked more green than blue in the soft twilight.

"Compliments? Does that mean I'm forgiven?" Ellery was half-joking, half not.

Jack's brows shot up. "Forgiven? For what?"

"Meddling in police business?"

Jack made a sound that didn't quite have the energy of a full snort. "Yeah, well... Peer pressure can be difficult to resist."

"Very funny."

"I thought so." There was a faint twinkle in Jack's blue-green gaze. He sniffed the air. "Something smells great. Is that you?"

"Eau de shrimp tacos."

"Wonderful. You should wear it always."

They were still smiling and joking as they headed back to the terrace, arms wrapped around each other's waists.

"How long can you stay?" Ellery asked.

"You're stuck with me for the night. Newport's CSI team is still excavating the basement at the Black House."

"And—?"

Jack opened his mouth, but was forestalled when Watson charged out of the grass, rubber frog squeaking madly, and delivered his prisoner to Jack's feet. "Hi, you rascal." Jack let go of Ellery, bent, picked up the frog and hurled it into the trees.

Watson cast him a reproachful look and bounded off.

"That should keep him busy."

"Dream on," Ellery said. "So? What have they found so far?"

Jack looked surprised. "What makes you think they've found anything?"

"Thirty police vehicles parked outside Black House for two days?"

Jack grimaced. "There are no secrets on this island."

"I wouldn't say that. Miss Blackwell kept hers for nearly a half-century." He remembered his conversation that morning with the still-s*lightly* chastened Nora. "*Oh*. I know now why everyone assumed Mrs. Parrish was Cressida's daughter."

"Why?"

"That's the story Miss Blackwell told her cook, who then told Gail McGillicuddy, the Bloodworth's cook, who told her niece Maggie, who's married to Detective Lansing."

"Great," Jack muttered.

"Then Maggie repeated the same story to Maria McGillicuddy. Maria used to clean house for Miss Blackwell, so it was kind of a self-perpetuating spiral. Everybody trusted their source, not realizing that the *original* source was Miss Blackwell."

By then they'd reached the terrace and the table set for dinner.

Jack studied the candles, the small bowl of flowers, the gold-rimmed china. "This looks serious." He was smiling that funny little smile he got sometimes.

Ellery said lightly, "I am serious." But maybe that was too much. Jack's eyes got that dark, grave look—the look that used to precede his telling Ellery he just wanted to be friends. "So?" Ellery prodded. "What has CSI uncovered so far?"

Jack made a face. "Not exactly dinner conversation."

"We're not eating." Ellery warned, "And we won't be until you tell me."

Jack raised his brows. "But you already know. Two skeletons buried in the brick wall. One male. One female. That's all anybody is willing to commit to at this point."

"They don't know the age of the skeletons? They can't tell how they died?"

"The age looks about right. There are no discernable injuries. But, like I said, they're still in the wall. We've got a forensic archeologist coming tomorrow. Until then, further excavation is on hold."

"Poison, I bet." Ellery couldn't help an inward shudder at the memory of all those cups of Pirate's coffee he'd swallowed.

"Maybe. But until the remains are out of the wall and into the morgue, we can't know for sure."

Ellery nodded.

"We did find boxes of women's clothing and accessories, a lot of it monogrammed, and some of it labeled *Cressida*."

"That's…"

"Sad," Jack said. "Sad and sick. What a waste of three young lives."

"I always knew Miss Blackwell was a little odd. A little eccentric. But she seemed harmless. I thought *she* was the one in need of protection."

"You're an actor," Jack said. "You know people aren't always what they seem."

"What about Sue?" Ellery asked. "What's happening there?"

"We'll have to wait and see. It's not up to me. Someone died during Sue's commission of a crime. A court will decide what punishment she deserves."

"Trespassing," Ellery objected. "It's not like she was robbing a bank."

Jack looked disapproving. "Unlawful entry is unlawful entry." That was probably a reminder for Ellery, but then Jack relented. "I don't see Sue doing jail time, if that's what you're asking."

"I don't have any desire to see Sue in jail." That was the truth. He didn't think Sue belonged in jail. Her printing press maybe—or possibly on a bonfire.

"Hey." Ellery suddenly smiled. "Did I hear you right? I've got you all to myself until tomorrow morning?"

Jack's smile was slow and a little wicked. His lips parted—

Arf. Arf. Arf.

Jack swallowed whatever he'd been about to say. He looked around for the source of that distant frantic barking.

"*Now* what's he dug up?" Ellery muttered.

"The case of the missing squeaky toy." Jack sounded half-resigned, half-amused.

Ellery said lightly, "Our next great adventure?"

"Uh no." Jack was grinning as he pulled Ellery back for another kiss. "Definitely not."

AUTHOR'S NOTE

Dear Reader,

Welcome once again to Pirate's Cove, where sinister shadows lurk behind every corner of our cute, quaint village. So many murders! Such a little police force!

Scandal at the Salty Dog is the fourth book in the Secrets and Scrabble M/M cozy mystery series. Because this series will likely prove my longest-running, the challenge becomes how to keep the murders, er, fresh for both readers and myself. Obviously every "villain" cannot be a criminal mastermind, a secret psychopath, or an unlikable rich person. Accidents happen. Sometimes good people do bad things. Sometimes bad people do good things. Variety is the spice of life—and death.

These stories are set on fictional Buck Island. The character of Watson is based on my own adopted pup Spenser (formerly known as Watson).

Thank you as ever to dear, dear Keren. Thank you to Kevin. Thank you to Emily-Bemily. Thank you to R.R.

Thank YOU, dear readers. I could not make this voyage without you.

BODY AT
BUCCANEER BAY

SECRETS AND SCRABBLE BOOK FIVE

DEAD MEN TELL NO TALES

Mystery Bookshop owner Ellery Page
and Police Chief Jack Carson
are diving for the sunken pirate galleon
Blood Red Rose when they discover
an old-fashioned diver's suit,
water-damaged and encrusted with barnacles.
Further examination reveals
the nineteenth century suit contains
a twenty-first century body.

Who is the mysterious diver?
No one seems to be missing
from the quaint and cozy town of Pirate's Cove.
Was he really diving for pirates' gold?
And if not, what exactly did he do
to earn that bullet hole in his skull?

ABOUT THE AUTHOR

Author of over sixty titles of classic Male/Male fiction featuring twisty mystery, kickass adventure, and unapologetic man-on-man romance, JOSH LANYON'S work has been translated into twelve languages. Her FBI thriller *Fair Game* was the first Male/Male title to be published by Harlequin Mondadori, then the largest romance publisher in Italy. *Stranger on the Shore* (Harper Collins Italia) was the first M/M title to be published in print. In 2016 *Fatal Shadows* placed #5 in Japan's annual Boy Love novel list (the first and only title by a foreign author to place on the list). The Adrien English series was awarded the All Time Favorite Couple by the Goodreads M/M Romance Group. In 2019, *Fatal Shadows* became the first LGBTQ mobile game created by *Moments: Choose Your Story.*

She is an Eppie Award winner, a four-time Lambda Literary Award finalist (twice for Gay Mystery), an Edgar nominee, and the first ever recipient of the Goodreads All Time Favorite M/M Author award.

Josh is married and lives in Southern California.

Find other Josh Lanyon titles at www.joshlanyon.com, and follow Josh on Twitter, Facebook, Goodreads, Instagram and Tumblr.

For extras and exclusives, join Josh on Patreon.

ALSO BY JOSH LANYON

NOVELS

The ADRIEN ENGLISH Mysteries

Fatal Shadows • *A Dangerous Thing* • *The Hell You Say*
Death of a Pirate King • *The Dark Tide*
Stranger Things Have Happened • *So This is Christmas* •

The HOLMES & MORIARITY Mysteries

Somebody Killed His Editor • *All She Wrote*
The Boy with the Painful Tattoo • *In Other Words...Murder*

The ALL'S FAIR Series

Fair Game • *Fair Play* • *Fair Chance*

The ART OF MURDER Series

The Mermaid Murders • *The Monet Murders*
The Magician Murders • *The Monuments Men Murders*

BEDKNOBS AND BROOMSTICKS

Mainly by Moonlight • *I Buried a Witch*
Bell, Book and Scandal

The SECRETS AND SCRABBLE Series

Murder at Pirate's Cove • *Secret at Skull House*
Mystery at the Masquerade • *Scandal at the Salty Dog*

OTHER NOVELS

This Rough Magic • The Ghost Wore Yellow Socks
Mexican Heat (with Laura Baumbach) • Strange Fortune
Come Unto These Yellow Sands • Stranger on the Shore
Winter Kill • Jefferson Blythe, Esquire
Murder in Pastel • The Curse of the Blue Scarab
The Ghost Had an Early Check-out
Murder Takes the High Road • Séance on a Summer's Night

NOVELLAS

The DANGEROUS GROUND Series
Dangerous Ground • Old Poison • Blood Heat
Dead Run • Kick Start • Blind Side

OTHER NOVELLAS

Cards on the Table • The Dark Farewell • The Dark Horse
The Darkling Thrush • The Dickens with Love
I Spy Something Bloody • I Spy Something Wicked
I Spy Something Christmas • In a Dark Wood
The Parting Glass • Snowball in Hell • Mummy Dearest
Don't Look Back • A Ghost of a Chance
Lovers and Other Strangers • Out of the Blue
A Vintage Affair • Lone Star (in Men Under the Mistletoe)
Green Glass Beads (in Irregulars) • Blood Red Butterfly
Everything I Know • Baby, It's Cold (in Comfort and Joy)
A Case of Christmas • Murder Between the Pages
Slay Ride • Stranger in the House

SHORT STORIES

A Limited Engagement • The French Have a Word for It
In Sunshine or In Shadow • Until We Meet Once More
Icecapade (in His for the Holidays) • Perfect Day
Heart Trouble • Other People's Weddings (Petit Mort)
Slings and Arrows (Petit Mort)
Sort of Stranger Than Fiction (Petit Mort)
Critic's Choice (Petit Mort) • Just Desserts (Petit Mort)
In Plain Sight • Wedding Favors • Wizard's Moon
Fade to Black • Night Watch • Plenty of Fish
Halloween is Murder • The Boy Next Door
Requiem for Mr. Busybody

COLLECTIONS

Short Stories (Vol. 1) • Sweet Spot (the Petit Morts)
Merry Christmas, Darling (Holiday Codas)
Christmas Waltz (Holiday Codas 2) • I Spy...Three Novellas
Dangerous Ground The Complete Series
Dark Horse, White Knight (Two Novellas)
The Adrien English Mysteries Box Set
The Adrien English Mysteries Box Set 2
Male/Male Mystery & Suspense Box Set
Partners in Crime (Three Classic Gay Mystery Novels)
All's Fair Complete Collection
Shadows Left Behind: An Historical Mysteries Box Set

CPSIA information can be obtained
at www.ICGtesting.com
Printed in the USA
BVHW051218040523
663580BV00016B/784